I0609220

Lucien Perey, Laura Ensor

Memoirs of the Princesse de Ligne

Vol. II

Lucien Perey, Laura Ensor

Memoirs of the Princesse de Ligne
Vol. II

ISBN/EAN: 9783337169039

Printed in Europe, USA, Canada, Australia, Japan

Cover: Foto ©Raphael Reischuk / pixelio.de

More available books at **www.hansebooks.com**

MEMOIRS

OF THE

𝔓𝔯𝔦𝔫𝔠𝔢𝔰𝔰𝔢 𝔡𝔢 𝔏𝔦𝔤𝔫𝔢

EDITED BY

LUCIEN PEREY

TRANSLATED BY LAURA ENSOR

IN TWO VOLUMES.—VOL. II.

NEW YORK

SCRIBNER AND WELFORD

1887

Printed by R. & R. CLARK, *Edinburgh*

CONTENTS

CHAPTER VII

CHAPTER VIII

CHAPTER IX

CHAPTER X

IV

THE Prince-Bishop at last decided to start
for Paris.   He had hardly arrived when he
received a visit from Madame de Pailly, who
informed him of his niece's inclinations, and
explained to him the progress of affairs.   The
Bishop earnestly requested to see the Princesse de Ligne-Luxembourg herself, but at
that moment she was staying with Madame
de Brionne at her country place of Limours.
Madame de Pailly at once resumes her pen:—

   "The Prince-Bishop, Madame, is always
inquiring whether you have returned; he is
extremely desirous to have the honour of

seeing you, and I should be very glad if you could seriously discuss the matter with him.

"Occasions on which I can prove to you my zeal and entire devotion will not be wanting with so vacillating a mind ; you will be able to say through me anything you please. I will see to everything, and render you a faithful account of what happens. But it seems to me that we must settle between ourselves what is to be the point of departure. He has referred several times to the question of settlements, especially with regard to the present. Would it not be better to present him with a copy of the deed of property? It would hurry on the transaction, and be a wise measure.

"The Prince de Salm's agents are very active ; he constantly alludes to him, and he listens to my replies as if they were quite new to him ; he goes on confiding to my ear all the proposals that are made to him. We have three fresh rivals, who, for the present, however, give me no anxiety."

The desired explanations at last arrived from Brussels, in the following letter :—

THE PRINCESSE DE LIGNE-LICHTENSTEIN TO THE PRINCESSE DE LIGNE-LUXEMBOURG.

" I trust, Princess, you do not doubt the tenderness of my feelings towards you ; the gratitude I now owe you can only increase it.

" I have the honour to enclose the paper concerning M. de Ligne's property. For the last year he has put all his affairs into my hands, and as I sign everything and collect all the revenues, and M. de Ligne even gives me the receipts for the money he draws from the estates, I can guarantee the exactness of the document.

" I am too sure of my husband's affection for you, Princess, and the confidence he has in your judgment, not to feel certain that he will agree to any arrangement you may choose to make for his son. I beg to entreat you, Madame, in case you should think an

income of twenty-five thousand livres [1] not
sufficient for the present, to fix the sum yourself, for I only require one more year to
settle the affairs of our house (public opinion
having kindly reported that they were in a
much more confused state than I found them
to be). I can promise you to honour any
arrangements and liabilities that you will
undertake for our young people. All they
will have to do when they draw their income every three months will be to sign
their names. I have made it a rule in business to consider as sacred the dates on which
income or pensions fall due.

" The affection I bear towards my children
leading me perhaps to overlook their faults,
it would ill become me to praise our son, but
I must believe the testimony of those who
knew him at Strasburg during several years ;
and at the present moment we have every
reason to be satisfied with the character he
bears in the army.

---

[1] One thousand pounds sterling.

" Pray, therefore, do not relax your kindness towards him, and let your efforts conduce to his happiness. You will also be contributing towards mine, for to see him settled and to be surrounded by my children will be my greatest joy.

"Receive, Princess, the assurance of my deepest respect and esteem," etc. etc.

This letter had a wonderful effect on the uncle, but did not move his niece.

"The young lady," writes Madame de Pailly, "is infatuated with M. de Salm; he has some emissary about her whom we do not know, and who demolishes beforehand all we can say against him. Even the Comte de Horn's name has been brought forward as an honour, on account of the Regent's phrase [1] about him.

"The good uncle feels his own weak-

---

[1] The Comte de Horn, a connection of the Regent through his mother, the Princess-Palatine, was condemned to death for murder. The family implored his pardon, appealing to the Regent on the ground of relationship. "When I have bad blood," the Regent coldly replied, "I have it drawn," and the pardon was refused.

It is probable that they boasted to Hélène of the connection between the Horn and Orléans families without mentioning the Count's crime.

ness, and carefully endeavours to hide it; he has agreed to everything with me, and, as I have been fortunate enough to persuade him, he fancies I shall have the same success with his niece, as if they were in the same frame of mind. To-day he is going to use all his influence, and at the same time inform her of the visit he wishes me to make, and of the entire trust he desires she should have in me. I shall lend myself to all his wishes, and shall have the honour of sending you a report of this interview. Receive, I pray," etc.

The uncle did not meet with the slightest success in his efforts to overcome his niece's resistance. Madame de Pailly was obliged to confess it to her correspondent: " There is one point, Madame, on which I think you will be obliged to give way; the Bishop asserts that he can only overcome his niece's passionate wish to be married in Paris by pledging his word that she shall spend three winters there under your guidance, so as to

get accustomed to the fashionable world. He
appears to attach great importance to this
promise; for he feels the great advantage it
would be to his niece. You still have time,
Madame, to think over this matter, for we
can discuss the other points in the meantime; I will tell you what they are when I
see you. . . ."

The Princesse de Ligne kept her nephew
informed of all these negotiations; as for the
Prince's father, he was still detained with the
army, waiting for peace to be signed. Prince
Charles wrote a short cold note to his aunt, in
which he did not even allude to his marriage:—

"MY DEAR AUNT—Although peace has
been declared the Congress is not yet over;
my father is very displeased at it; he is still
in a wretched village, feeling very dull, with
nothing to do.

"He will certainly go to Paris as soon as he
can; I envy him the pleasure he will have in
seeing you, my dear aunt.

" Allow me to assure you from time to time
of the feelings of affection and respect with
which I remain all my life," etc. etc.

The coolness the Prince displayed will be
easily understood when we learn that he already felt for a friend of his childhood a love
which was never completely effaced. But, accustomed as he was absolutely to respect the
paternal or rather the *maternal* will, it never
entered his mind for one moment not to
obey.

His mother had eagerly agreed to their
cousin's plans. Hélène's large fortune, the isolated position of the young girl, which would
tend to make her adopt her husband's family
as her own, had quite won over the Princess, who ignored or pretended to ignore her
son's secret affection. She therefore perse-
vered in her efforts, hoping to succeed, though
the object in view was not easy to attain.

The Bishop of Wilna had been won over
to the de Lignes, but he had many a hard

battle to fight, for an unforeseen circumstance had strengthened Hélène's resolution not to leave Paris. Her friend, Mademoiselle de Lauraguais, had married the Duc Auguste d'Aremberg, cousin of the de Lignes, who, like him, resided for part of the year at the Court of Brussels. The young Duchess returned to Paris for some time, and at once visited her former companions at the Abbaye-aux-Bois. She had heard of Prince Charles' proposed marriage, and gave Hélène a most gloomy description of life in Brussels. The latter immediately repeated this to her uncle, making the picture several shades darker. The poor Bishop did not know who to listen to ; in the midst of his perplexities he determined to despatch the Abbé Baudeau, who was always at hand, to Bel Œil,[1] giving him instructions to confer verbally with the Princesse de Ligne on the delicate subject of a residence in Paris, as well as on the money

---

[1] Bel Œil was the summer residence of the Princes de Ligne, and will often be referred to later on.

question.   He was allowed great latitude on this latter point, and accordingly set off.

Madame de Pailly lost no time, and again wrote to the Princesse de Ligne-Luxembourg: "We have had news of the envoy, Madame, and we hear he is much pleased with everything, but he sends word that Madame la Princesse de Ligne will not hear of a three years' residence in Paris.

"The Bishop appeared to me very much disturbed at the effect this would have on his niece, as she had always held to this condition.   You know there is nothing more difficult to overcome than the fancies of a young person, and unfortunately she has been confirmed in this one by all that Madame d'Aremberg de Lauraguais has told her. The Abbé will arrive perhaps to-day; I shall be there, and we will first work upon the uncle, so as to make him work upon his niece.

"M. de Salm will not give way ; he has sent his picture to his friend at the Convent, and she has invited the Princess Hélène to a collation, given in a room of which this portrait forms the chief ornament.

"I was at the opera with a lady who is much interested in this fine gentleman, and she said : 'What does it signify whether you are a scamp or not when you have a name and a large fortune ? Look, for instance, at so and so,' etc.

"God forbid that such morality should enter the head of our prelate and his niece. In the meantime I amused myself last night by quietly challenging my free-spoken young friend to tell me all the naughty stories about this charming Prince. The good Bishop bore it with a slightly embarrassed air, which quite amused me.

"I shall have the honour, Madame, to give you an account of the envoy's return, and of all its consequences. I beg you not to be impatient, and to rely on my zeal and my intense desire to do all that is agreeable to you.

" Receive," etc.

It was not long before the Abbé returned, and, though he had not succeeded in obtaining the promise of a residence in Paris, he had done much to push the matter forward. He brought magnificent fruit and flowers to the young Princess from Bel Œil, and in the description he gave of the almost regal magnificence of the place he neglected none of the details which were likely to charm and flatter her vanity.   He had granted handsome pecuniary conditions, and the Princess, on her part, had seemed disposed to accept the marriage - contract proposed by the Abbé.

MADAME DE PAILLY TO THE PRINCESSE DE LIGNE-LUXEMBOURG.

"All is going on wonderfully well, Madame; you will find the Prince and his envoy very well satisfied.   At dinner we had a melon from Bel Œil, and peaches were sent to the Princess Hélène.   I proposed the health of

the giver ; but they will tell you the rest.   I
am rejoiced at the position of affairs.

"The Abbé may have every possible fault,
but he confirms me in my opinion that one
can do nothing with fools and everything
with intelligent people.   The young Princess
is converted, and her good uncle, agreeing to
the Abbé's expedient, says : 'It will cost
me thirty thousand livres[1] a year more to
make my niece happy.   I will do it, Madame,
if only you are satisfied.'"

The Princesse de Ligne - Luxembourg
wrote to her cousin to give her this good
news, and to urge her to come to Paris as
soon as possible ; but she was in no hurry,
and, like a prudent mother, wished above all,
to settle everything relating to the income and
household arrangements of the future young
couple, for whom she dreaded certain tempta-
tions, from which she herself had suffered.
She again sent her steward to Paris with two

---

[1] Twelve hundred pounds sterling.

letters, one of which was a confidential one to her cousin.

BEL ŒIL, 19*th January* 1779.

" I despatch you my steward, Princess ; he will have the honour of handing you this letter, and I have instructed him to carry out exactly whatever you are kind enough to order.

"The Prince arrived at Vienna on the 5th of June ; I therefore think he will soon be home again, in which case I should only go to Paris with him, or even a couple of days later, if I can possibly avoid going before.

" In any case, Princess, I shall await your orders.   I reserve myself the pleasure of assuring you personally of all my gratitude. I have never doubted the success of anything which you were good enough to take in hand.

"As our young people will not have to receive, and as the ordinary expenses of the household cannot possibly absorb all their income, I fear that too large a fortune may be hurtful to them, and lead perhaps to gambling, or other extravagances, which would do them harm, and which they would always consider themselves obliged to increase in proportion to their income ; especially when they will come into their respective fortunes. I look at this matter from a mother's point of view. Pray do not let it go beyond the family."

The Princesse de Ligne-Luxembourg told the Bishop of her cousin's wise advice, but no attention was paid to it. The Congress of Teschen was over, and the Prince de Ligne was returning home slowly, for he always found much to delay him on the road. We will not inquire into the nature of these delays ; he, however, found sufficient time to write a few lines from Vienna to his cousin, and to the Bishop of Wilna, which he had neglected doing for the last two months.

TO THE PRINCESSE DE LIGNE-LUXEMBOURG.

"I am told, Princess, that, thanks to your kindness, all is going on well, also that you have done me the honour of writing to me. . . . I have not received anything. They say I must write to the Bishop. I beg you will give him the enclosed letter.

"If you have any commands to give me, address them to the Post Office at Munich; I shall find them in passing through.

"All the information I receive from Poland appears to coincide with our views.

"I place myself at your feet, Princess, and beg to assure you that my gratitude is equal to my tender and respectful attachment.

"LE PRINCE DE LIGNE."

A few days after the receipt of this letter they had agreed upon all points; a draft of the settlement was drawn up, and the Princesse de Ligne and her son announced their arrival.

In spite of the very small inclination the young Prince felt for this marriage, he experienced a certain curiosity to see his future bride. As for Hélène, she was far more interested in her outfit, her presents, and her diamonds than in her husband. Among other things, she had been promised "certain girandoles [1] and diamond bracelets of wonderful beauty—old family jewels, that she was most impatient to see, and she was in a great fright lest they should be left behind at Brussels." Her future aunt undertook to explain this childlike anxiety to the wife of the steward, so that she might remind the Princess to bring these precious trinkets. She answered as follows :—

"On my return home I found a letter from the Princess, announcing her immediate arrival, and adding that she is bringing with her the girandoles and the bracelets ; so the Princesse Hélène need have no cause

---

[1] Large diamond earrings that were worn with the Court dress.

for anxiety. I shall have the honour of paying her my respects on Monday. We have
also heard, through M. le Comte Tasson, that
M. le Prince de Ligne will reach Brussels,
at the latest, on Monday. I hasten to apprise
your Highness of the fact, and beg she will
accept the assurance of deepest respect," etc.

The Princesse de Ligne's first visit was
to her cousin. She there found the Prince-
Bishop awaiting her arrival. After a long
conversation and endless compliments on
either side, it was settled that the Bishop
should escort the Princess and her son to
the Abbaye-aux-Bois.

Hélène, who had been warned the day
before, was very much vexed at having to
make her first appearance in her school dress ;
but no exception could be made to the rule.
She went down to the parlour accompanied
by Madame de Sainte Delphine, and very soon
perceived that the plainness of her dress did
not prevent the Prince from thinking her very

pretty. Though she pretended to cast her
eyes modestly down during the visit, she took
care to see enough of her future husband to
be able to say to her companions on returning :
" He is fair, has a tall slight figure, and re-
sembles his mother, who is very handsome ;
he has a noble mien, but he is too serious, and
there is something German about him !"

The Prince's father arrived three days
later.

" I abandon M. de Ligne to your indignation, Princess," his wife writes to their cousin ;
" you may prepare her for his arrival, which
will certainly be either to-day or to-morrow ;
it fills me with the greatest joy !"

The Prince-father had his head completely
turned by his future daughter-in-law, who did
all she could to please him, intuitively feeling
that he was the one with whom she could
best sympathise.

Having no family in Paris, it was decided
that Hélène's marriage should be celebrated
in the chapel of the Abbaye-aux-Bois, to the

great delight of the pupils. The Bishop gave
his niece an outfit worth a hundred thousand
écus ;[1] the wedding casket, offered by the
Lignes, was provided by Léonard ; the laces,
ordered at Brussels and Mechlin, were real
masterpieces of work.   The jewels offered to
Hélène, besides the family diamonds and the
famous girandoles, were chosen by herself at
Barrière's and at Drey's. She gave a trinket
to each of her companions in the red class,
and a magnificent luncheon, *with ices*, was
given by the Prince-Bishop to all the pupils,

---

[1] The Princesse Hélène received as her marriage-portion
Mogylani, an estate with a residence and country-houses, two
palaces at Cracow and one at Warsaw.   Prince Radziwill owed the
Massalski family a sum of one million eight hundred thousand Polish
florins, inherited through Hélène's mother.   He had given them as
interest three important estates, of which half the income belonged
to Hélène, and the other half to her brother.   The Prince-Bishop
promised to give and guarantee the Princess, from her wedding-
day, a clear income of sixty thousand livres, payable in Paris, and
to pay all their expenses in the event of their remaining in that city.
On the other hand, the Prince de Ligne promised to give his son,
on his wedding-day, a revenue of thirty thousand livres, and in
addition to lodge the pair at Brussels, or Bel Œil, or Vienna, in
one of his palaces or residences.   If they had any children, at the
end of four years the Prince promised to double the sum of
money.

including the *little blues*, who each received in addition a bag of sweetmeats.

The marriage-contract was signed at Versailles by their Majesties and the royal family, the 25th of July 1779. The wedding took place on the 29th at the Abbaye-aux-Bois.

It is needless to add that Hélène's nurse, Mademoiselle Bathilde Toutevoix, took part in the festivities. She adorned her pretty mistress to the very best of her ability, and the poor girl's head was so completely turned with joy that she even forgot her cockades.[1] She came down to the parlour after the bride, and modestly hid herself in a corner. Prince Charles approached her, and slipped into her hand his wedding present—an annuity of six hundred livres.[2] Hélène was much touched with this attention. " I thanked him," she says, "by a smile and pressure of the hand, the first I had granted him."

---

[1] She was in the habit of bedizening herself with them, and Hélène does not forget to mention in her memoranda that on that day she forgot them.

[2] Twenty-four pounds sterling.

The bride was led to the altar by her uncle, and by the Marquise Wielopolska, who took the place of her mother. The Duchesses de Choiseul, de Mortemart, de Châtillon, de la Vallière, etc., were present at the ceremony. The young Princess, exquisitely lovely in her bridal dress, fully satisfied the company by her "decent attitude, which was full of feeling" (style of that day). After receiving the congratulations of the brilliant assembly, Hélène went up to her apartment to change her costume; but, instead of returning immediately to the parlour, she quickly made her way to the choir chapel, where Madame de Rochechouart was buried, and kneeling on the tomb of the one who had been to her as a mother, she offered up to God her last girlish prayer. When she returned to the parlour she was rather pale, and her eyes showed signs of tears; but at the gates of the Abbey a post-chaise, drawn by six chafing horses, was awaiting; the postilions, in the pink and silver livery of

the Prince, being scarcely able to hold them ;
Hélène, after a rapid farewell, was hurried
into the carriage by her young husband, and
they started at full gallop for Brussels.

V

THE young couple first established themselves at Bel Œil, the magnificent summer residence of the Prince de Ligne. The Marshal was passionately attached to this regal abode, on which his father had lavished several millions. The property was composed of a succession of gardens, forests, parks, mansions, and shooting boxes, which the Prince de Ligne had designed with the most perfect taste. It was here that he preferred receiving his guests, and that he successively entertained the Prince de Condé, the King of Sweden, the Comte d'Artois, Prince Henry of Prussia, etc. Hélène was dazzled by the splendour of her new abode. A brilliant reception had been prepared in her honour. On the very day after her arrival, which had taken place in the evening, the young Princess, on opening her windows, perceived an immense park full of villagers elegantly attired as shepherds and shepherdesses, their dresses more like those of Watteau and Lancret than those commonly worn by the Flemish peasants. The Prince's dragoons were making merry at tables on the lawn; and a little farther off, in a grove, might be seen puppet shows, in another tight-rope dancers; a rural ballroom was established on a green sward; under a leafy bower a magician was distributing sham ointments in little boxes, which contained sweetmeats and trinkets. In another spot a bard was gaily reciting verses, composed by the Prince in honour of the newly-married pair; and if the composition was not brilliant in versification, it yet could boast of grace and art sufficient to compensate for its defects; finally,

Aufresne and Préville, who had arrived that same morning from Paris, were playing improvised proverbs in the private theatre of the residence. The festivities lasted the whole day ; after dinner the proverbs were replaced by a comedy in one act, with interludes of song, entitled, *Colette and Lucas*, composed by the Prince de Ligne in honour of his daughter-in-law.[1] The audience was composed of brilliant officers and fine ladies, who had come expressly from Brussels and even Versailles for the occasion. The play, though worthless, was courteously applauded ; but another had been prepared in order to compensate the spectators. Night having come on during the representation, sudden floods of light springing up in brilliant sheaves between the trees greeted the guests as they emerged from the theatre, and in the thickets fairylike illuminations lit up the arbours ; it was im-

---

[1] This comedy was printed in the private press at Bel Œil in 1781. The only copy known to be extant is in H.R.H. the Duc d'Aumale's library at Chantilly.

possible to see the lamps, cleverly hidden under the foliage. "It was not night," says Hélène : "it was silvery daylight."

The married couple appeared enchanted one with the other, with a shade more of tenderness on the part of the Prince. Hélène's beauty, grace, and intelligence surprised and charmed him ; he had not expected to find these qualities united in the person of a child of fifteen. Every one was under the same impression, and the Dowager-Princess herself, who was not easy to please, wrote as follows, some time after the wedding, to the Princesse de Ligne-Luxembourg :—

BEL ŒIL, 20th August 1779.

"Again I renew my thanks, Princess, and reiterate the expressions of gratitude I owe you. Our child is most charming, docile, and gentle, having no will of her own, and amused at everything ; in fact all that could be desired in a daughter-in-law if she were moulded by one's self. She has been quite a success with all who have seen her in these parts.

"As our children have both had the honour of writing to you, I will not, for fear of repetition, give you the details of our journey. Moreover, his Grace the Bishop of Wilna will have told you all; he appeared himself very well pleased with our country. Do try, Princess, to make him send my son his niece's portrait, in whatever style he prefers, even if it be that little pencil drawing we saw at the Abbaye-aux-Bois; and do not doubt, Princess, of the tender sentiments," etc. etc.

The Prince-Bishop had indeed been delighted with his stay in Flanders; the amiability of the family of Ligne, the harmonious relationship existing between its members, the distinguished intelligence and the kindness of Prince Charles in particular, all contributed to assure him of his niece's future happiness. He left her thoroughly satisfied.

For the first time Hélène was going to be

acquainted with family life; she could not
have had a better beginning, for the Lignes
lived together with an intimacy full of ease,
gaiety, and tenderness.   In her convent life
the little Princess, with the selfishness natural
to children, had only thought of herself, and
was not accustomed to the daily sacrifices
made by brothers and sisters, which are
made easy and rewarded by a mother's ap-
proval and kiss.   She had a serious appren-
ticeship to undergo.   She preferred her
father-in-law and the Princess Clary, her
sister-in-law, to all the other members of her
family.   The Princess Clary, the Prince's
eldest and favourite daughter, "his masterpiece," as he called her, was kindness, grace,
and affability itself.   Married some four years,
gifted with sound judgment and perfect tact,
she would have been an affectionate and
charming guide to her young sister-in-law at
the outset of her married life; but it was not
possible for her to assume this position, which
naturally devolved upon the Princess-mother,

who, jealous of her rights, would have ceded
her authority to no one.

The Princesse de Ligne played an important part, if not in the heart of her husband, at least in his household. The Prince
willingly rendered justice to his wife's qualities; he was full of consideration for her,
and treated her always with amiable defer-
ence. " My wife," he said, " is an excellent
wife, full of delicacy, feeling, nobility, and
in no way selfish. She is often in a pet,
but her temper soon passes away, melting
in tears and leaving no trace, for my wife
has an excellent heart." It was not difficult
for the Prince to resign himself to his wife's
temper, for it affected him very slightly.
Such was not the case with her children;
it must, however, be admitted that she had
often good cause for her unevenness of temper.
Not only was her husband constantly and
openly faithless to her, but he also squan-
dered his fortune, and in spite of the large
revenues he possessed would often have

been involved in serious difficulties had it not been for the watchful care of the Princess, who by her clever administration established a proper balance between their income and expenditure. However, in spite of the Princess's rather uncertain temper, the unvarying cheerfulness and good humour of the Prince made it a delightful home, for he possessed the rare quality of being as charming at home as in society.

Hélène thoroughly enjoyed her new life, and eagerly threw herself into the pursuit of pleasures entirely new to a little schoolgirl. She at once learnt to ride. Dressed in an elegant riding-habit, made to display her delicate and supple figure to perfection, and accompanied by her husband, she would spring into the saddle the first thing in the morning, as light as a bird, and as pleased with her liberty ; then three or four times a day, with childlike glee, she would array herself in new dresses from Léonard or Mademoiselle Bertin ; and we may be sure that they in no way resembled

the little black convent-frock. At all the
entertainments given in honour of her
wedding, she fascinated everybody by her
grace and liveliness; she danced with such
spirit, acted so naturally and with so much
animation, sang with a voice so youthful and
fresh, that her husband, though not sharing
her worldly tastes, was happy in her pleasure,
and allowed her to give herself up to it without
restraint.

Immediately after her arrival Hélène was
presented at the Court of the Netherlands.
The Ligne family possessed a magnificent
palace at Brussels, near the Cathedral of
Sainte Gudule, and often resided there during
the winter. At that time the Viceroy was
Prince Charles of Lorraine; he had married
the Archduchess Marie-Anne,[1] sister of Marie-
Thérèse, and was now a widower.

---

[1] This brave and clever prince was a most unfortunate general.
Beaten by the Prussians in 1742, while commanding the Austrian
army in Bohemia, he was again defeated in Alsace in 1745. The
affability of his manners, his artistic and literary tastes, his kindness
of heart, endeared him to all, and his paternal rule is still

The Prince of Lorraine often came to hunt at Bel Œil. " He could not help being kind, even in his fits of temper, which were rare. One day, for instance, while hunting, on which occasion he gave himself the airs of an old huntsman, enraged at a number of people who disturbed the hunt by overrunning the forest at Bel Œil, he called out : 'Go to the devil!——if you please, gentlemen,' he added, taking off his hat."

The liveliest, wittiest, and most fashionable man at the Court of Brussels was certainly the Prince de Ligne's father, and he enjoyed his life there extremely. " It was," he says, "a nice Court, gay and at the same time secure, idle and agreeable, with plenty of drinking and hunting." However, when the Duke

remembered in Belgium. His generosity was boundless, and the con siderable income he received (six hundred thousand florins of Brabant) did not suffice to cover his expenses. He ruined himself by his prodigality, but science and art prospered under him, and schools of paintings and colleges were established in every town. New roads were made ; trade, then at a low ebb, received a fresh impulse ; and a transport service was organised between the Flemish ports and those of Germany and France.

held a levee, and invited ladies, nothing but the most inoffensive gaiety was permitted, for the Prince hated all license and bad taste.

Prince Charles's palace at Brussels was an immense and ancient building. Brussels reminded one somewhat of Paris, the town offering every kind of resource. The *cours* was the favourite promenade, and there the grandest equipages were to be seen. The coachbuilders of Brussels were famous, and the Duke was anxious that the nobility should possess the most elegant specimens of their work. Hélène made her first appearance on the *cours* in a superb gilt coach made by Simon; all the panels were delicately painted, in the most beautiful *vernis Martin*,[1] by clever Viennese artists.

In spite of his love for the Court of Brussels and his passion for Bel Œil, the Prince never stayed very long at either; he generally started off at a moment's notice.

---

[1] A species of lacquer painting, at present revived in France.

"What a charming existence mine was, in my dear and delightful Bel Œil. In twenty-four hours' time I could be either in Paris or in London, at the Hague, at Spa, etc. Once I went to Paris to spend one hour there, and another hour at Versailles, after the Queen's last confinement : *I saw her on the fourth day*," he carefully adds.

"On another occasion I took all my company there to the opera in a coach of my own."

It was natural that the Prince should like Paris and Versailles, for he was the soul and life of the little intimate circle around the Queen ; his presence gave animation to everything, and his invariable good humour and sallies of wit always secured him a smiling welcome. He was to be seen everywhere, arranging or disarranging the gardens ; presiding at entertainments and directing the illuminations : he took part in the Queen's lansquenet, Mesdames' cavagnole, Monsieur's whist, the Prince de Condé's quinze, the King's game of billiards, and the Prince de Conti's pharaon.[1] He said everything that came into his head; but although he gave way to much exaggerated merriment, from time to time, under cover of a joke, he would make many serious truths acceptable.

His great friends were the Polignacs,[2] whose intimate society consisted of the Coignys, the Conflans, the Comte de Vaudreuil, and the Chevalier de l'Isle. He always defended the Polignacs against the numerous accusations which were brought against them.

He writes: "There is no one more virtuous and more disinterested than all these Jules, but their company was some-

---

[1] All different games of cards, in vogue at that time at the French Court.

[2] The Duchesse de Polignac, Gabrielle - Yolande - Martine de Polastron, an intimate friend of the Queen, was both amiable and beautiful. Expressive blue eyes, a high forehead, a nose very slightly turned up, a lovely mouth, with pretty little white teeth which were beautifully symmetrical, formed a most agreeable physiognomy. Her features bore the stamp of sweetness and modesty. At the age of seventeen she married the Comte Jules de Polignac.

times monotonous, so great was their fear of giving rise to prating and gossip; the Comtesse Diane was the only one whose conversation was at all lively."

The Prince was particularly intimate with the Chevalier de l'Isle,[1] the least known member of the little circle.   The Chevalier was an excellent officer, an encyclopedist, and a poet, a correspondent of Voltaire[2] and also of the Prince de Ligne, who held him in great esteem.   He was a master of song, and reigned supreme in the art of letter-writing. He had never composed a faulty verse, or written a letter that was not both witty and in excellent style; however, in society he was wanting both in good taste and breeding, giving way to ill-temper and familiarity.

---

[1] The Chevalier de l'Isle was a brigadier in the King's cavalry, having been appointed on 25th July 1762. Very intimate with the Choiseul family and Madame du Deffant, he is mentioned in the latter's correspondence.

[2] It was he who wrote a letter to the patriarch of Ferney about a badly-executed commission commencing as follows : " You must, sir, be very stupid," etc.   This beginning threw Voltaire into an ecstasy of delight.

So as to make believe that he dined with the Queen at the Polignacs on Sundays, he would arrive the first after dinner, that those who came after him should be deceived by this manœuvre. He wrote regularly to the Prince about all that went on at Versailles during his absence. The following is an example of his letters :—

16th January 1780.

"What a turkey we have just eaten at the Comtesse Diane's! My goodness, what a fine bird! M. de Poix had sent it from the poultry-yard. There were eight of us round it : the lady of the house, Madame la Comtesse Jules, Madame d'Henin, and Madame de la Force ; M. le Comte d'Artois, M. de Vaudreuil, the Chevalier de Crussol, and myself.

"While we were eating the turkey, but without reference to it, some one mentioned you, my Prince. Stay, let me recall who it was ? A lady——no ; a man—yes, certainly a man, for he said *Charlot*, and our ladies are not given to such familiarities. It was the man who was on Madame la Comtesse Jules' left hand. Let me see; I was next to the poet; here sat the Chevalier de Crussol, and there M. de Vaudreuil, and then——Ah! now I've got it, it was M. le Comte d'Artois; yes, I am sure of it now. He said: 'By the bye, who can tell me if Charlot has arrived at Brussels?'—'I can, your Highness, for I have received four lines in his own handwriting, and am myself going to write to him; who has any message to send?' All immediately answered in a chorus: 'I have, I have, I have.' In the confusion I could distinguish these words: 'I embrace him, I love him; tell him to come, we expect him.' When the hubbub had subsided the soft voice of Madame la Comtesse Jules commenced more audibly: 'Tell him that if he had dated his last letter more distinctly, I would not have failed to answer it; but that, although assisted by

several experts in the art of deciphering, it
was impossible for me even to suspect from
what place it had been written, and conse-
quently to what place I should direct my own.'

"Thereupon we conversed about you,
and then about Admiral Keppel, then
of the turkey, then of the capture of
our two frigates, then of the Spanish In-
quisition, then of a large gruyere cheese
which our ambassador in Switzerland has
just sent his children, then of the strange
conduct of the Spaniards towards us, and
at last of Mademoiselle Théodore, who,
upon my life, dances better than ever, and
who pleased us yesterday as much by her
talent as Mademoiselle Cécile by her youthful charms. To-morrow the Queen will
receive for the first time; till now she has
only seen those who have the '*petites en-
trées*'; she is rather thinner, but otherwise
her health leaves nothing to be desired.
The King is still the good husband, the good
father, and the good man he has always

been; it is impossible to be near him without admiring him as the personification of honesty, and without being sincerely attached to his person. I assure you we are fortunate in possessing such a royal couple : may God preserve them on the throne where His goodness has placed them! . . . We are all going to-morrow to Paris to inaugurate the charming little house M. le Duc de Coigny has bought, and in which we shall have—— What do you think we shall have?—— Our first grand entertainment—a regular house-warming. We shall have farces, proverbs, verses, songs, and pleasures of all kinds; it will be a beautiful ceremony.

"*À propos* of verses : you have not seen those I wrote the other day for the Queen, threatening to play her the trick she most dreads—that is, to name her at the opera ball. Here it is :—

> "Dans ce temple ou l'incognito
>   Règne avec la folie,
> Vous n'êtes grâce au domino
>   Ni reine in jolie.

Sous ce double déguisement
Riant d'être ignorée,
Je vous nomme et publiquement
Vous serez adorée. [1]

" I implore you, Prince, my very dear Prince, do not massacre my song in honouring me by singing it yourself; leave that care to my cousin, who will give it its full value; love her for me, and tell her I shall go to Brussels, on my head if necessary, to see her; you must love me, both of you."[2]

The Queen was an object of devotion to the Prince de Ligne. " Who could

---

[1] In this temple, where incognito
Reigns as well as folly,
You are, thanks to the domino,
Neither queen nor beauty.
Under this twofold disguise,
Laughingly unknown,
Should I name you, then at once
You will be publicly adored.

[2] In order to elucidate this paragraph, we must explain that the Prince sang dreadfully out of tune, and that the pretended cousin was the lovely Angélique d'Hannetaire, daughter of the director of the theatre at Brussels; she sang beautifully, and was very intelligent; the Prince was madly in love with her at that time.

see the unfortunate Marie Antoinette without adoring her ?" he writes thirty years later.[1] " I only realised it the day she said to me : ' My mother is displeased at your remaining so long at Versailles ; go and spend some days at your post ; from thence write letters to Vienna, in order to show where you are, then come back.' Such kindness, such delicacy on her part, and still more the idea of having to spend a fortnight without seeing her, drew tears from my eyes ; but the charming heedlessness, which preserved her from all coquetry prevented her noticing my emotion.

"As I do not believe in a passion which cannot be reciprocated, a fortnight was sufficient to cure me of a sentiment I now admit for the first time, and which, for fear of ridicule, I never should have confessed to any one else. . . . Have I ever seen in her society anything that did not bear the impress of grace, kindliness, and good taste ?

---

[1] See *Fragments of unedited Memoirs of the Prince de Ligne,* published in the *Revue Nouvelle.* Paris, 1840.

She intuitively knew an intriguer miles off, and hated every kind of deceit; that is why she preferred the society of the Polignacs and their friends—that is to say, Valentine Esterhazi, Bésenval, Vaudreuil, Ségur, and myself."

If the Prince worshipped the Queen, on the other hand he had little esteem for the King. He writes: "The King—in whom I hoped to find some good qualities, whom it may be said I have protected, whose mind I have endeavoured to elevate by interesting discourses, instead of his hunting topics or idiotic conversation—cares for nothing but tomfoolery. His practical jokes are always aimed at Conflans, Coigny, or the Polignacs' friends. The Queen has managed to cure him of this habit. It was at bedtime that his Majesty liked to worry us. He possessed, however, a certain tact in the midst of his rough jokes. One day, when he was threatening us with his blue ribbon, which he tried to throw at some one's head, the Duc de Laval withdrew. The King said: 'Do not fear,

Monsieur; it has nothing to do with you.'
. . . Coigny, the eternal fault-finder, said to
me one day : 'Would you like to know what
these three brothers are ?   A fat locksmith,
the wit of a country public-house, and a
street fop.'   The two last epithets applied to
Monsieur and the Comte d'Artois."

When the Prince returned to Bel Œil he
delighted his youthful daughter-in-law with
these tales ; for although she liked Flanders
fairly well when not there alone with her
mother-in-law, she could not help regretting
Paris, when her husband's duties recalled him
to the army, and her fickle father-in-law went
off on his incessant travels.

It will be remembered that the Dowager-
Princess had absolutely refused to consent to
a residence in Paris during the winter months.
She was right, for although the officers
generally returned to their respective capitals
during the bad season, the military profession
did not allow much leisure time, and Prince
Charles, being in the Austrian service, would

scarcely have been able to spend his leave in Paris. The young Princess would therefore have been left to the care of an aunt, who had no authority over her, or to that of a father-in-law, more absorbed in amusing himself than acting as mentor to his daughter-in-law. This delicate and dangerous position had naturally alarmed the Princesse de Ligne, but Hélène had not such foresight; the pleasure she anticipated of appearing in the brilliant society of which she had only just caught a glimpse outweighed any feelings of prudence, and she quite hoped to obtain her husband's consent in the matter.

The first step consisted of her presentation at Court. Hélène had gained an ally in her aunt the Princess, who was quite ready to conduct her pretty niece to Versailles; but the latter wished to make her appearance there with all the honours of war—that is, with those of the *tabouret*.[1] This could only be

---

[1] To have the right of sitting down in the King or Queen's presence.

obtained by virtue of certain rights. The
rank of grandee of Spain was a sufficient
title. The Prince de Ligne possessed this
rank, and Hélène persuaded her husband to
ask the Prince to make it over to him. Such
a request was not a small affair. The young
Prince was rather embarrassed, the more so
that this request would entail another, that of
a grant of money. Magnificent costumes and
jewels, etc., had absorbed the largest part of
the young couple's income. However, incapable of refusing any wish of his wife's,
Prince Charles took heart, and decided upon
writing. He immediately received from his
father, who was then at Versailles, the most
charming reply :—

VERSAILLES, 10*th September* 1780.

" Is it not, my dear Charles, a droll thing
to be married ? You will manage to get
on, for, after all, one is bound more or less
according to circumstances. It is only fools
who do not know how to turn the position to account : meanwhile you have a very

pretty little wife, whom without false shame you may love. Although from father to son we have been called Lamoral, without knowing whether he is a saint, I am neither moral, moralist, nor moraliser enough to preach, and I make fun of those who do not believe in my morality, which consists in trying to make all around me happy. I feel quite sure that this is your case also; without having a whole array of principles, this is one of the four or five I have adopted as a second education : my first, as I told you, is, that to be a liar or a coward would bring me with sorrow to my grave. Certainly, my dear fellow, you have well understood this short lesson.

"And now, let us come to business. Take as much money as you require ; my men of business must have it or obtain it ; that is one subject done with. . . . The Queen said she will make my affair de Kœurs[1]

---

[1] An estate of the Prince de Ligne in France, and about which he had a lawsuit ; the name of the estate is pronounced like *cœurs* (hearts), hence the Prince's pun.

a success, and, when I told her that my *affaires de cœur* (love affairs) were successful, she said *I was a fool.* Kœurs settled, that makes two affairs done with. Your uncle, the Bishop of Wilna, who fancies that you or I may some day be King of Poland, wants us to obtain the *indigénat* ; we shall get it, that is another affair terminated.

"Our aunt of the Tuileries wants your wife to have the *tabouret;* she has a fancy for going to Versailles, and for that purpose wishes me to cede to you the *grandezza.* I have already written to the King of Spain and to the minister on the subject, and have spoken of it to the ambassador. Fourth affair concluded, leaving me the prospect of taking cold, by being obliged to get down at the gates of the Court, where only the coaches of the grandees of Spain are allowed to enter, as in the Luxembourg and elsewhere.

"Here are two sources of economy for me!—the King's play and *coucher,* which no longer cost me anything.

"What annoys me is to hear clever people say foolish things; to hear war discussed by idlers, who have never seen anything but military exercises, and those badly done; disinterestedness proclaimed by women who manage to get pensions by dint of torment-ing the ministers and the Queen, who is a thousand times too kind; to hear sensi-bility professed by those who have had at least twenty lovers. And then, the in-triguers! the obtrusive! and the wicked! How often this makes my blood boil, but a quarter of an hour later I forget it all.

"Shall I tell you a foolish saying of mine, considered as such by all the royal family? You know that at the town theatre I am under the King's box, amongst the public; you will remember the mirror in *La fausse Magie*.[1] At the close of the play it was dreadfully cold, and the King complained of it, as well as of the coldness of the acting. I

---

[1] *The false Magic*, a comic opera by Grétry.

said : 'It is because the *dénouement* is *à la glace*.'[1]   The two brothers[2] hooted me out loud for this pun.   This existence at Versailles is delightful; it is like life in a country-house.   I embrace your wife and your mother for having had wit enough to make me a Charles like yourself.

"*P.S.*—By the bye, I had already planned in my head a grove for my Charles, a fountain that will bear the name of Hélène, and a bower for their children.

"I shall work at it as soon as I leave Versailles, to go and tell you, *tutti quanti*, that I love you with all my heart."

---

[1] A pun on the word *glace*, which in French means either ice or a looking-glass.

[2] Monsieur and the Comte d'Artois.

VI

THE Prince had not spoken lightly when he
said to his son that they would go to Poland
for the *indigénat*.[1] In the midst of all the
pleasures and amusements of Versailles he
suddenly departed. " Family interests," he
says, "obliged me to undertake a long journey.
My son Charles has married a pretty little
Pole, but her family has given us paper in
lieu of hard cash. Their claims were on the
Russian Court; it was necessary to go and
present them. In June 1780 I started for

---

[1] The *indigénat*, though differing from naturalisation, conferred
on those who obtained it all the privileges belonging to those in-
digenous to the soil.

Vienna, Prague, Dresden, Berlin, Saint
Petersburg, Warsaw, Cracow,—where I had
much to do,—Mogylani,[1] Léopol, and Brunn,
—where I was in love.   I must not forget to
add that I started from Paris and the Rue de
Bourbon, from the house of the Duchesse de
Polignac, who had just been confined,[2] and
where I had dined with the Queen.   I
promised to return at the same hour in six
months' time, and ordered my livery coach
and courier in consequence."

The sum of money the Prince de Ligne
claimed in the name of his daughter-in-
law was considerable.   It amounted to four
hundred thousand roubles, which were well
worth the trouble of recovering.   However,
we incline to the belief that these family
affairs were merely a cloak for political designs ; the journey was probably intended to
carry on the preliminaries of a negotiation

---

[1] An estate belonging to the Princesse Charles.
[2] The Duchess had given birth to the Comte Armand-Jules de
Polignac on 14th May 1780.

begun by Joseph II. and the Empress
Catherine in their interview at Mohileff.
The Prince started from Vienna, whither
he had gone to receive his final instructions.
His companions on the journey were his son
Charles, and his friend the Chevalier de
l'Isle.

" I made de l'Isle a colonel," he says, " by
simply saying when in Austria, Prussia,
Poland, and Russia that he was one, and
buying him a pair of epaulets. I was also
obliged to knight him," he adds, " in order
to distinguish him in foreign parts from
the Abbé of the same name."[1]

The Princes started on their journey a
year after the war of the Bavarian succession had ended. " This war entailed on
the King of Prussia a large expenditure of
men, horses, and money ; it procured him
an appearance of honesty and disinterested-

---

[1] The Abbé Delille, born at Aigueperse on 22d June 1728,
died in Paris on 1st May 1813. He was a member of the French
Academy, and as a poet enjoyed European celebrity. Though spelt
differently the name was pronounced in the same way.

ness, and some political amenities, but it brought him no military honour, and caused him to entertain very bitter feelings towards us. Without any apparent reason the King forbade Austrian officers to enter his dominions without a special permit signed by him. The Austrian Court retaliated by making the same rule with regard to Prussian officers. This gave rise to mutual discomfort without reason or profit. Being of a confiding nature, I thought I could do without a permit, but the desire to have a letter from the great Frederick, rather than the fear of being badly received, induced me to write to him."

Instead of one letter the Prince de Ligne received three, all charming. For fear of missing him the King had written from Potsdam to Vienna, Dresden, and Berlin. The travellers arrived at Potsdam on the 28th of June.

" Having to wait until twelve o'clock, at which hour I was to be presented to the King, together with my son Charles and M.

de l'Isle, I went to the parade ground, and was soon surrounded and escorted by Austrian deserters, especially those from my own regiment, who tried to fawn upon me and ask my forgiveness for having left me. The hour for the presentation arrived, and the King received me in the most charming fashion. The military stiffness of headquarters was exchanged for a tender and benevolent welcome. He said he did not know I had so old a son.

"'He has even been married a year, Sire.'

"'May I ask to whom?'

"'To a Pole—a Massalski.'

"'What, a Massalski? Do you know what her grandmother did?'

"'No, Sire,' replied Charles.

"'She fired off the cannon at the siege of Dantzic,—she fired, and made them fire, and defended the place, when her party, who had lost their heads, only thought of yielding.'

"'Women are unaccountable creatures,' said I, 'strong and weak by turns, cautious and dissimulating, they are capable of anything.'

" 'No doubt,' said M. de l'Isle, annoyed at not having been spoken to, and he added, with a familiarity which met with no success, ' See, for instance——'

" The King interrupted him at the end of half a second.   In order to satisfy de l'Isle I told the King that M. de Voltaire had died in his arms ; so that the King asked him a few questions.   He answered rather too lengthily, and went away.   Charles and I remained for dinner.

" Every day the King had long conversations with me, often of five hours at a time, and completely fascinated me: fine arts, war, medicine, literature and religion, philosophy, moral philosophy, history and legislation, were all reviewed in turn.   The great eras of Augustus and Louis XIV. ; the refined society of the Romans, the Greeks, and the Franks ; the chivalry of Francis the First ; the frankness and valour of Henry the Fourth ; the revival of learning ; anecdotes of clever men of former days, and their failings ; Voltaire's errors,

Maupertuis's irritability, and I know not what
else.   In fact, anything and everything.
The most varied and wittiest things were
said by the King in a soft, low, and agreeable voice, with an inexpressibly graceful
movement of the lips.   The charm of his
manner was, I think, the reason why one
did not notice that, like Homer's heroes, he
was rather a babbler, though certainly a sublime one.   His eyes, always too hard in his
portraits, although strained with work and
the fatigues of war, softened in their expression when listening to or relating some
noble deed or trait of sensibility. . . .

  "One morning, as I arrived at the palace,
the King came forward and said : 'I fear I
must be the bearer of bad news ; I have just
heard that Prince Charles of Lorraine is
dying.'   He looked to see what effect the
news would have on me, and seeing the tears
fall from my eyes, he gradually and gently
changed the conversation.   The next day,
the moment he saw me, the King came up,

and said with an air of the deepest con-
cern : 'Since you must hear of the death of
a man who loved you and honoured man-
kind, it is better that it should be through
some one who feels it as sincerely as
I do; poor Prince Charles is no more!'
He was deeply affected as he said these
words."

After a conversation during which the
King had spoken unceasingly for nearly an
hour, the Prince, finding the part of listener
rather monotonous, seized upon an allusion
to Virgil, and said :—

"'What a grand poet, Sire, but what a bad
gardener!'

"'How true! Did I not try to plant,
sow, dig, and hoe, with the Georgics as
my guide? "But, Sire," the gardener used
to say, not knowing who I was : "You are
a fool, and your book also; it is not so
that one sets to work." Good heavens,
what a climate! would you believe it, God
and the sun refuse me everything! Look

at my orange, olive, and lemon trees, they
are all dying of hunger.'

"'Laurels, I see, are the only trees that
will grow for your Majesty.'

"The King gave me a delighted look,
and to cap my insipid remark with a bit of
nonsense, I quickly added: 'And then, Sire,
there are too many grenadiers[1] in this country,
they swallow up everything.'   The King
laughed, for it is only nonsense that makes
one laugh."

The Prince knew that the King could
not bear M. de Ried, and that it was because the latter had mentioned the taking
of Berlin by Marshal Haddik that the King
had conceived such a dislike for him; therefore, when Frederick asked him if he found
Berlin much altered, he took care not to remind him that he was one of those who took
possession of it in 1760.   "He was pleased
with my reticence, for he was an old wizard,

---

[1] *Grenadiers* in French signifying both the soldier and the
pomegranate tree.

who guessed everything, and whose tact was the finest that ever existed."

The Prince asked him a bold question when speaking about France.

"There is everything, Sire, in that country, and it really deserves to be happy; it is reported that your Majesty had said that if one wished to have a happy dream, one ought——"

"Yes," interrupted the King, "that is true—one ought to be King of France."

After spending a delightful fortnight at Potsdam, the Princes took leave of the King of Prussia with regret, and continued their journey, arriving at Saint Petersburg in the month of August.

The Empress received the Prince de Ligne with the greatest distinction; she was already acquainted with him through Voltaire's letters and the accounts the Emperor Joseph had given her at Mohileff. Catherine found him worthy of all the praise she had heard of him, and writes:—

" We have also the Prince de Ligne, who is one of the most amusing and easy beings to get on with I have ever seen. Though an original and a deep thinker, he yet has all the gaiety of a child. His company would suit me very well."

On his part the Prince was charmed with Catherine the Great, as he called her, and, thanks to his account, we have a living portrait of the Czarina.

" It was easy to see that she had been handsome rather than pretty ; the majesty of her brow was softened by a pleasant look and smile, but it showed all the force of her character, and revealed her genius, justice, judgment, courage, equanimity, gentleness, calmness, and firmness.

" Her chin, though rather pointed, did not exactly project ; nor was it a receding chin, but one nobly proportioned. The oval of her face was not good, and yet it was pleasing, for the expression of her mouth was full of frankness and mirth. She must have had a fresh complexion and a fine bust, which, however, she got at the cost of her figure; she had been almost too slight, but one becomes very stout in Russia. She was clean, and if her hair had not been drawn so far back, but allowed to surround her face, she would have been better looking. One did not notice she was small; when she told me, in a slow manner, that she had been very vivacious, it seemed impossible to realise it. On entering a drawing-room she always made the same three bows, like a man, in the Russian style; one to the right, one to the left, and the other in the middle. Everything about her was measured and methodical."

The Prince had already become very intimate with Catherine at the end of a few days.

"' What did you suppose I would be like?' she asked me.

"' I fancied your Majesty tall, stiff as a poker, with eyes like stars, and a large hoop. I thought also I should only have to admire, and constant admiration is very fatiguing.'

"' Is it not true that you did not expect to find me so stupid ?'

"' In truth, I thought it would be necessary to have all one's wits about one, that your Majesty allowed yourself all license, and was a perfect firework of wit; but I infinitely prefer your careless style of conversation, which becomes sublime when treating of noble passages of history, or examples of sensibility or greatness.' And the Empress heartily laughed at this clever mingling of frankness and flattery.

" It was this contrast of simplicity in what she said with the great deeds she performed that made her interesting. A trifle amused her ; she was pleased at the smallest joke, and cleverly turned it to account. One day I told her that to silence the reproaches of a lady who was displeased with my scarcity of talk, and looking bored in her house, I replied that I had just heard of the death of an aunt who had brought me up.   When the Empress was bored on the grand reception days, she would say to me : ' My uncle is about to die.'   Then I would hear it murmured : ' We are going to have a mourning.'   And all the Court would search up the uncle in the almanac, and of course not find him."

However great the fascination Catherine exercised over the Prince, she did not make him forget Marie-Thérèse, and towards the end of his stay he wrote : " The Empress Marie-Thérèse had certainly much greater charm and fascination.   Our Empress carried one away : the impression made by the Russian Empress was much weaker at first, but gradually increased.   However, they resembled each other in this, that if the universe had crumbled away they would have been found *impavidas ferient ruinæ*.   No power on earth would have made them yield ; their great souls were proof against adversity ; enthusiasm preceded the one and followed the other."

It was, however, necessary for the Prince to tear himself away from the delights of this charming abode.   But before their departure the Empress, laughing, said to the Prince-father: "As you told me that you would either sell, gamble, or lose any diamonds I should give you, here are only a hundred roubles' worth round my portrait on this ring!" [1]

To this present Catherine added jewels for the Princesse de Ligne and her daughters; Prince Charles received a rich casket for Hélène, and the Princes left for Poland, having forgotten only one thing, viz. the claim of four hundred thousand roubles, for which they had undertaken their journey.

---

[1] It is said that Catherine's *friendship* for the Prince de Ligne became a warmer sentiment, and we are disposed to believe it when we read the sour letters that Grimm wrote to the Empress about the Prince, of whom he was jealous.   It will be seen later on that he excited Potemkin's jealousy as well.   Be this as it may, the Prince was very discreet on the subject, as also on that of the political conversations he had with the Empress, for he relates nothing about them, not even in reference to Poland.   We can hardly believe, however, that he did not touch upon the subject ; the Princesse Charles was Polish, and Catherine might well suppose that her father-in-law and husband took some interest in that un-happy country.

"For," says the Prince gaily, "it seemed to me a want of delicacy to take advantage of the favour with which I was received to obtain favours."

The Bishop of Wilna received the Prince at his residence of Werky, a short distance from Warsaw. "Werky," writes the Prince, "was a fortunate child of nature,—a large river, three smaller ones, and a chain of mountains, separated two valleys. Four or five waterfalls, three islands, manufactories, castles, a windmill, a port, a ruin, two convents of handsome appearance, natural undulations, temples to Vulcan, to Bacchus, and one to Unity, which is to be erected upon piles, and a kind of bridge at the meeting of three pretty rivulets, an obelisk, a fisherman's and a workman's hut, bridges, some ornate, others rustic, complete the attractions of this magnificent estate. I advise and direct everything."

The Dietine (sub-Diet) of Wilna had assembled to elect deputies for the Diet of

Warsaw. The Bishop gathered round his
table eighty-four Polish gentlemen, nearly all
wearing the national costume, and having
their heads shaved after the Polish fashion.
Before dinner each of them came up to salute
the Bishop by respectfully kissing the hem of
his robe. At the end of the repast healths
were drunk; the Bishop proclaimed the name
of the person whose health was proposed;
then he filled an antique cup, beautifully
chased, emptied it and turned it over, showing
that he had drained it to the bottom. He
then passed it to his right-hand neighbour,
and in this way it went round the table.
These toasts were always celebrated with
champagne or Tokay. After an interesting
sojourn at Werky and Wilna, the Princes,
accompanied by the Bishop, started for Warsaw. We have seen that in the negotiations
for the marriage of the Duc d'Elbœuf with
Hélène the Prince-Bishop and the Marquis
de Mirabeau had dreamt of the Polish throne
for the young Princess's future husband. This

idea had taken possession of the Bishop's brain; and the accounts that were given to him of Saint Petersburg, and the peculiarly cordial reception that the Princes had received, confirmed him in it.   Persuaded that the Prince was far advanced in the Empress's good graces, and convinced that the King Stanislaus - Augustus was no longer in favour, the Bishop, ever ready to throw himself into a new adventure, took advantage of the opening of the Diet to propose the Marshal as candidate for the *indigénat*.

"You will one day be King of Poland," said the enthusiastic Bishop; "what a change will come over European affairs! what good luck for the Lignes and Massalski!" The Marshal laughed, but, although he ridiculed these sayings, he allowed matters to proceed. "I had a fancy," he says, "to please the nation assembled for the Diet, and accordingly presented myself."

Twenty-five candidates came forward to

obtain the *indigénat;* twenty-four of them were set aside, the Prince alone was retained ; but it required a unanimous vote, and three opponents came forward. " They were nearly cut down, and the violence of one of the nuncios,[1] who laid his hand on his sword, uttering very threatening words, nearly broke up the Diet, and my too zealous partisan had a narrow escape of losing his head.

" I sought my opponents ; I succeeded in overcoming their prejudices, and that so thoroughly that they said, with a grace and eloquence worthy of their country, that, in favour of an acquisition they considered so honourable, they would, each in turn, solicit the vote of one of their friends. Against all custom, I rushed into the nuncios' hall, and embraced the mustachios of these three orators. It electrified me, for I began an oration myself—in Latin too! then I took them by the hand, and my advances resulted

---

[1] The Polish deputies were called nuncios.

in a general *sgoda*,[1] which rang three times
through the hall, nearly bringing it down, so
great were the universal acclamations."

After having obtained the good graces of
the Empress Catherine, laid out the Bishop
of Wilna's gardens, gained the *indigénat*, and
become almost as popular at Warsaw as in
Brussels, the Prince de Ligne, faithful to his
word, arrived at Versailles to the very day,
six months after having left it.

---

[1] The *sgoda* was the cry which announced the unanimity of the
vote.

VII

HÉLÈNE awaited her husband's return with the greatest impatience, for during his absence and that of his father her life had not been an easy one.

The Dowager-Princess generally took advantage of her husband's absence to reduce the expenses of her household, and re-establish, as much as possible, a condition of things too often upset by the Prince, who, like the amiable spendthrift that he was, gaily threw millions out of the window. Hélène would gladly have taken her share in superintending the household; for she had learnt at the Convent how to keep house, and was naturally proud of her acquirements. She gracefully proffered her services to her mother-in-law, anxious to display her domestic qualities, but the Princesse de Ligne was not disposed to share her authority with any one, and coldly refused her daughter-in-law's offer. Hélène, rebuffed and humiliated, did not complain, but it left a feeling of rancour in her mind, and from that moment the relations between mother and daughter-in-law became more strained. At last the Prince's six months' journey drew to a close, and it was with twofold joy that Hélène hailed her husband's return, and the end of the harsh tutelage under which she had been living.

The Princes found their family at Brussels, and in the spring went to Bel Œil, where they spent the summer together, with the exception of Prince Louis, who was detained by his service in Paris, and could seldom be with them. The life at Bel Œil was extremely gay and animated; the

stream of visitors was incessant, and poured
in from all sides — Brussels, Paris, and
even Vienna. The officers of the de Ligne
regiment came to stay in turns. Not only
did the Prince keep open house—that is to
say, that people could come and spend the
day there without any previous warning, but
there was also a certain number of apartments
kept in readiness for any unexpected guests
who might come for a longer visit. Among
the intimates at Bel Œil were the most
charming women of the Court of Brussels.

Although the de Lignes provided ample
entertainment and amusement for their
guests, a due part of the day was devoted
to more serious occupations. The morn-
ings were given up to study. Music, literature, drawing, etc., were cultivated in turn.
"Christine pastes and unpastes, Hélène sings
and is enchanting," wrote the Prince. As
for him, he was no sooner up than, book in
hand, he went to his island of Flora, or
worked in his library, or else inspected the

gardens. He already possessed a private
printing-press in his house at Brussels; he
installed another at Bel Œil, which was a
source of great amusement.[1] Prince Charles
in particular busied himself with it, but he
confined himself to publishing the works of
others; his father, the Chevalier de l'Isle, and
the Abbé Payez, provided ample material for
the small presses of Bel Œil.

Prince Charles, who was an enthusiastic
admirer of pictures, had found time, in spite
of his studies and military duties, to make a
magnificent collection of original drawings,
both of ancient and modern masters.[2] He
was a thorough connoisseur, and drew well
himself, he even undertook to engrave
some of the drawings in his collection, and

---

[1] The volumes printed at Bel Œil are extremely rare and much
in demand. M. Adolphe Gaiffe is in possession of one of the two
known copies of the Chevalier de l'Isle's poems. From a memo-
randum left by the Princess, we believe that part of her childhood's
Memoirs was printed by her husband at Bel Œil.

[2] A catalogue of them was made by Adam Bartsch in 1794; it
contained six thousand numbers.

sent for the celebrated Bartsch to give him
lessons at Bel Œil. Hélène interested herself in her husband's occupations, and, while
he was engraving, put the drawings in order,
studied under his guidance the different styles
of each master, and became quite an en-
lightened amateur. These intellectual occupations took up the first half of the day,
after which the family and numerous visitors
assembled for dinner. After an hour's rest
they all went into the gardens, where they
wandered about, or indulged in reverie, or
gathered together according to taste. There
were a hundred different pastimes, and a
hundred different ways of enjoying one's self;
the Prince had anticipated every taste and
every wish. Sometimes they went long
excursions on horseback or in carriages to
the beautiful forest of Baudour, adjoining the
woods of Bel Œil, or they sailed on the
large lake which was connected with the
canals, rivers, and smaller lakes of the park.
The boats were decked out with streamers,

and manned by small boatmen dressed in the Prince's livery. " During the lovely summer evenings," he writes, "our excursions on the water, with music and a bright moonlight, were most agreeable to the ladies."

The Prince never forgot them in his rustic arrangements ; well beaten-paths, so that they might not wet their pretty feet, bowers of roses, jasmine, orange trees, and honeysuckle, led to the ladies' baths. They found shaded benches and rustic cabins, and also "their embroidery frames, their knitting, their netting, and, above all, their black writing-books. Sand or something else was often wanting, but they contained secrets unknown both to lovers and husbands, and, used as desks by their owners, served to write many a pretty little lie."

At this period Brussels presented the most brilliant and animated aspect. Prince Charles of Lorraine had been succeeded by the Arch-

duchess Marie-Christine, formerly Regent of
Hungary, whereshe had enjoyed the privileges
of a queen.   She held her court on a grand
scale, and did the honours of it with grace
and affability.   The Archduchess was considered the handsomest of Marie-Thérèse's
four daughters.   She danced so gracefully
and so lightly that, directly she began, every
one stopped to admire.   Although pretending
to be annoyed, she was, on the contrary, far
from displeased at the admiration she pro-
voked.   She had married the Archduke Albert
of Saxe-Teschen,[1] who was entirely under his
wife's influence, and, unlike Prince Charles of
Lorraine, never gained the hearts of the Flemish.   Nevertheless, the Archduke's gentle and
easy character made him beloved by all who
approached him.   He was an intelligent
connoisseur in pictures, and formed two

---

[1] Son of Augustus III., King of Poland ; and Field-Marshal in
the Austrian army.   He was born on 11th July 1738, and married,
on 8th April 1766, Marie-Christine-Josepha-Jeanne-Antoinette,
sister of the Emperor Joseph, born on 13th May 1742.   She died
in 1798, and the Archduke Albert in 1822.

magnificent collections of paintings and drawings.

The Archduchess and her husband took pleasure in encouraging art and literature, and Brussels soon became a lively literary centre. All that appeared in France—novels, poetry, travels, etc.—was eagerly read. Several reviews were started. The Prince de Ligne welcomed young Belgian authors, and helped them in every way to the best of his ability. Happy to avail themselves of the lordly hospitality he so graciously offered, they constantly came to submit to him their essays. It is needless to say that they extolled the beauties of Bel Œil and Baudour in verses which were reproduced in the gazettes of the day.

If Belgium had not become the scene of political events, it is probable that the Prince would have founded a school of literature and good taste, for he occasionally evinced in his writings talent of the highest order. Ideas flowed in abundance from his fertile pen, and he seemed merely to jot them down on the paper at haphazard. His style, which is capricious, incorrect, and even obscure, is always lively and descriptive; each word seems to fall naturally into its place under his pen; wit abounds, unexpected, satirical, and sometimes most daring. He has the greatest contempt for grammar; but this very negligence, this lordly indifference, gives to his writings a most original style.

Moreover, he possessed all the requisites of an excellent critic, but it must be acknowledged that he was blindly indulgent towards his own poetry. Unfortunately gifted with deplorable facility, he never missed an opportunity of rhyming. One evening, when they had all gone for a long walk in the woods, they wandered so far into the forest that they completely lost their way, and only found it, thanks to a star Hélène had noticed. On the following day her father-in-law brought her a ballad, set to a tune then in vogue, and perhaps among all those he has written, it may be considered as one of the best :—

À HÉLÈNE.

Air: Sous la Verdure.

Un sombre voile
Nous dérobait notre chemin ;
Nous errions à la belle étoile,
Mais nous arrivons à la fin
    Grâce à l'étoile.

    Est-ce l'étoile
Qui jadis guida vers un Dieu ?
Ou de Vénus est-ce l'étoile ?
Je penche beaucoup en ce lieu
    Pour cette étoile.

    Auprès d'Hélène
Conduit l'étoile du berger ;
Trop heureux celui qu'elle amène
Tout juste à l'heure du berger
    Auprès d'Hélène.[1]

And so the days passed quickly and pleasantly, the only drawback in this happy

---

[1] To HÉLÈNE.

A dark mist
Concealed our road ;
We wandered in the open air,
But at last we reach our goal,
    Thanks to the star.

scene being the state of Hélène's health,
which required an amount of care her youth
and love of pleasure made it difficult for her
to take. Two accidents had successively
destroyed a hope dearly cherished by her
husband, and even more by her father-in-
law, who was anxious that his beloved
Charles should have a son. The waters of
Spa, then very much the fashion, were recommended. Hélène went there in the
month of May 1782, accompanied by the
Chevalier de l'Isle, and her convent friend,
Mademoiselle de Conflans, who was now
Marquise de Coigny,[1] and on intimate terms

Was it the star
That formerly led us heavenwards?
Or was it of Venus the guiding star?
I am disposed to believe
That it was this latter star.

'Tis to Hélène
That this star led us,
Too happy he that by it brought,
Comes just at the happy moment
Near to Hélène.

[1] It was to this witty Marquise de Coigny that the Prince de
Ligne addressed the charming letters written from Tauris.

with the de Lignes.   Hélène wrote to appoint a meeting-place.   The Chevalier de
l'Isle, who had a ready pen and familiar
style, answered as follows : " Madame de
Coigny embraces Mouchette,[1] and exhorts
her to wait for her to go to Spa till the
fifteenth of next month."   Hélène waited for
her, and they started together with the
Chevalier ; he only remained a short time,
and on his return wrote to the Prince de
Ligne : " I did not write to you from Spa, my
dear Prince, because I hoped to see you
there, and then because I intended stopping
at Brussels, at Bel Œil even ; I had begged
the Princesse Charles, who talks much better
than I can write, to speak to you of me in
her spare moments.   She has none ?   So
much the better for both her and you, and
so much the worse for me.   But I had my
turn at Spa ; twenty times I was on the
point of writing, if only to tell you how

---

[1] Familiar nickname of the Princesse Charles.

charming your daughter-in-law was, and then I reflected that you were not the man to ignore it, and that when one has nothing fresh to say, one had better hold one's tongue."

Shortly after the Chevalier's departure the Prince rejoined his daughter-in-law at Spa.

A watering-place at that time was very much like what it is in our days, but the Prince describes it in the most spirited manner : " I arrive in a large hall, where I find the maimed showing off their arms and their legs; ridiculous names, titles, and faces; clerical and worldly animals jumping and running races; hypochondriac *milords* wandering sadly about ; females from Paris entering with roars of laughter, to make one believe they are amiable and at their ease, and hoping thereby to become so ; young men of all countries, counterfeiting the English, speaking with their teeth closed, and dressed like grooms, their hair cut short, black, and greasy, with a pair of Jewish whiskers surrounding dirty ears.

"French bishops with their nieces; an accoucheur, decorated with the order of Saint Michael; a dentist with that of the Spur; dancing and singing masters in the uniform of Russian majors; Italians in that of Polish colonels, leading about young bears of that country; Dutchmen scanning the papers for the rate of exchange; thirty so-called Knights of Malta; ribbons of all colours, to the right and the left, at the buttonhole on both sides, orders of all kinds, shapes, and sizes.

"Old duchesses returning from their walks armed with tall canes *à la Vendôme*, and three coatings of white and rouge; marchionesses, cheating doubly at cards; horrible and suspicious faces, surrounded by piles of ducats, and swallowing up all those that were timidly put on the large green cloth; two or three electors in hunting-dress, striped with gold, armed with hunting-

knives ; a few princes incognito, who would
not produce a greater sensation under their
own names ; some old generals and officers
retired on account of wounds they never
received ; a few Russian princesses with their
doctors, and Palatines and Castilian ladies
with their young chaplains.

"Americans and burgomasters of the
neighbourhood ; convicts escaped from all
the different prisons in Europe ; quacks of
every description ; adventurers of all kinds ;
abbés of all countries.   Twenty sick people
wildly dancing for their health ; forty lovers,
or pretended lovers, sweating and agitating
themselves, and sixty feminine waltzers of
more or less beauty and innocence, cleverness
and coquetry, modesty and voluptuousness.
All this combined is called a dancing break-
fast."

After leaving the establishment of the
mineral waters, the Prince takes us to La
Sauvetière, an elegant meeting-place for
bathers : "The noise, the buzzing sound of

conversation, the uproar of the music, the intoxicating rhythm of the waltz, the passing and repassing of the idlers, the oaths and sobs of the gamblers, both men and women, the weariness of this magic-lantern made me leave the hall. I sit down, and I see some water drinkers religiously counting their glasses and their steps, and congratulating themselves, perhaps rather sadly, on the improvement of their digestion. Some ladies join their group.

" ' Do you digest the waters, Madame ?'

" ' Yes, sir, since yesterday.'

" ' Does your Excellency begin to digest?' she says to the minister of an ecclesiastical court.

" ' I have the honour to inform your Excellency,' he answers, 'that I perspire from eight o'clock in the evening till ten, and that I sweat completely from ten till midnight. If I had not so much business to transact for his Grace, I should be entirely cured by the treatment.' "

Hélène returned to Spa in 1783, and met there Madame de Sabran, born a d'Andlau,[1] who became later the Marquise de Boufflers. She was one of the most charming women of her time, and pleased every one who saw her by her appearance, her elegance, and the kindliness of her nature. She was accompanied by her little son, Elzéar de Sabran, who little thought of the part he was destined to play in politics later on; for the present, he contented himself with learning the part of Chérubin in the *Mariage de Figaro*, the Princesse Charles studying Suzanne, and Madame de Sabran the part of the Countess, for after the return from Spa the play was to be acted at Bel Œil.

Just at this time they received news of the Comte d'Artois' arrival in Flanders,[2] and

---

[1] Madame d'Andlau was daughter of the famous Helvétius and Mademoiselle de Ligneville. She had educated her daughter, Madame de Sabran, very well: Madame d'Andlau in no way shared her father's opinions.

[2] We read in the *Gazette des Pays Bas*, dated Thursday, 17th July 1783: "On Monday, H.R.H. the Comte d'Artois, ac-

the Princes de Ligne started off at once to receive and accompany him on his progress through Rocroi and Spa, bringing him back with them to Bel Œil.

The Princesse Hélène returned to Bel Œil before the Princes, in order to prepare for the Comte d'Artois' reception ; but he had barely arrived when he fell seriously ill. The Prince had prepared festivities which cost him over fifty thousand francs ; he never even spoke of them to the Count, who was not in a condition to enjoy them.   Only one thing took place, a fairy-like illumination of the park, which the Prince, however, did not see, for he never left the Comte d'Artois' side, and started with him for Versailles.

After the departure of the Comte d'Artois, the Chevalier de Boufflers and Madame de Sabran came to Bel Œil.   Hearing that the

companied by their Excellencies the Governors-General, saw all that was remarkable in the vicinity. The next day the Prince, with their Royal Highnesses, left for the Chateau de Marimont, from whence he was going to Bel Œil."

Chevalier was garrisoned at Valenciennes, the Prince wrote and proposed his joining him at Tournai, and from there returning with him to Bel Œil. The Chevalier replied : " I am very much tempted, my dear Charlot, by all you suggest ; but on closely examining your marching orders, I believe that my regiment is the very thing I should miss. Tell me when you go to Tournai ; I intend going there, and defying you at the head of your army, and if I find it on two *Lignes* (lines), I shall try to break through them.

"Dear Prince, I love you as if I saw you every day of my life. After yourself there is nothing that gives so much pleasure as the impression that you leave. Send me your marching orders, so that we may meet somewhere, and that, if possible, we may part nowhere." [1]

---

[1] The Prince de Ligne had a particular affection for Boufflers. It would appear, however, that the Chevalier had a very uneven temper, for Madame de Sabran, in one of the charming letters she wrote him, gives us the following sketch : " It is not your manners, which are those of a savage, your absent and moody appearance,

The Chevalier arrived at Bel Œil in time
to take part in the representation of the
Mariage de Figaro, which was given with
great success in the pretty theatre at Bel
Œil. Hélène took the part of Suzanne;
Madame de Sabran that of the Countess;
Elzéar, Chérubin, and Boufflers, Figaro; as
for the Prince-father, he had to content
himself with the modest part of Doublemain,
the notary's clerk; we must confess that,
though he gave others[1] good advice, he acted
very badly himself. He was generally given
the part of the notary who draws up the
marriage-contract, or that of the lackey who
brings in a letter, and would invariably come
in at the wrong moment; but on the other
hand, once on the stage he would not leave
it, but say in a supplicating whisper to the

---

your sharp and genuine wit, your large appetite, and your deep
sleep whenever one wishes to converse with you, which made me
love you to distraction. It is I know not what : a certain sympathy
that makes me think and feel like you, for under that rough ex-
terior you conceal the spirit of an angel and the heart of a woman."

[1] See his *Letters to Eugénie on Theatricals*. Paris, 1771.

other actors : " I am not in your way, am
I ?"

Hélène acted with an archness and
vivacity which recalled the merry schoolgirl
of the Abbaye-aux-Bois, tempered by a little
experience ; the little Elzéar was charming
as Chérubin, but the Chevalier carried off the
palm by the zest and spirit with which he
threw himself into his part. It was a curious sight, and a sign of the times, to hear
Figaro's soliloquy recited by a nobleman,
and applauded by the aristocratic audience
of Bel Œil.

Prince Charles willingly lent himself to
his wife's amusements, though he took no
active part in them ; but his serious mind
required occupations of a different order. He
took a keen interest in all scientific dis-
coveries, and at that moment was much
taken up with the new process of aerostation
invented by Charles Pilatre de Rozier and
Montgolfier. He witnessed the first experi-
ments made in Paris, and among others the

ascension of a fire balloon, in the gardens of La
Muette, on the 21st of November 1783, made
by Pilatre de Rozier and D'Arlandes. The
aeronauts were in the greatest danger, their
balloon having caught fire ; they managed to
extinguish it, and made their descent at
Gentilly in safety. At that time a balloon
ascension was looked upon as a most daring
undertaking, and no one cared to accompany
the aeronauts. But Prince Charles, whose
courage and coolness were proof against
everything, determined to take part in the
third ascent, which took place at Lyons on
the 19th of January 1784. The seven
passengers were: the elder Montgolfier,
Pilatre de Rozier, Fontaine, Prince Charles,
and three other persons who at the last
moment wished to ascend. Although the
balloon was of enormous size, the number
of passengers was too great ; De Rozier had
foreseen this, and did not wish the two last
persons to enter the car. Montgolfier persuaded him, however, to let things be ; but

they were hardly off, and had only run about
five hundred fathoms, when the balloon
began imperceptibly to tear, and they were
obliged to make a hasty and perilous descent
at a distance of about a league from the town.
On their return to Lyons they were received
with acclamations by the whole population.
In April 1784 Prince Charles sent off from
the public square in front of the hôtel des
États, at Mons, a magnificent balloon, constructed at his own expense. He had invited
the Duke and Duchess of Aremberg and a
great many distinguished personages of the
Courts of Brussels and Versailles, who, after
the ascent of the balloon, all returned to Bel
Œil.[1]

---

[1] See the *Gazette des Pays Bas*, Monday, 5th April 1784, No.
xxviii.

VIII

THE Prince de Ligne and his daughter-in-law were in entire sympathy. The young Princess enjoyed living at Bel Œil when her father - in - law was there, but she disliked Brussels, their winter residence. We already know, by her own confession, that Hélène was as "obstinate as the Pope's mule," and she had not given up her purpose of settling in Paris. Her husband disliked the idea of the Paris life, so little in harmony with his tastes ; he had never lived in France, and, a stranger there, he feared comparison with the supreme elegance, the light witty tone, which distinguished the brilliant gentlemen at the Court of Versailles. But, as the saying goes, "What woman wills, God wills;" Prince Charles ended by giving way, and he bought in September 1784 a fine mansion, situated in the Rue de la Chaussée d'Antin.[1]

It is needless to say with what delight Hélène went to live in Paris. She found most of her old convent friends, and, presented under the auspices of her father-in-law, she was welcomed and entertained on every side.

Received everywhere into the most brilliant circles—at Chantilly, the Prince de Condé's; at Petit Bourg, the Duchesse de Bourbon's; at the Temple, the Prince de Conti's—all welcomed the young Princess, who gave herself up entirely to a vortex of pleasure and success. Captivated by the charm and amiability of the young men who surrounded her with their attentions, Hélène gave way to her natural instinct of coquetry; she distinguished no one

---

[1] This hotel occupied the whole of the space between the Rue de Provence and the Rue de la Victoire.

in particular but tried to please all; when
at home, she was occupied with her toilet
and saw very little of her husband, who but
rarely accompanied her into society, absorbed
as he was in his studies.   The steady character of the Prince, his taste for study, and
the very German and romantic turn of his
mind, formed a marked contrast with the
light, bantering, superficial tone assumed by
the courtiers.   Hélène, with the giddiness of
youth, decided in her own mind that her
husband was tiresome, and had it not been
for fear of offending her father-in-law she
would not have spared him a little bantering.

Prince Charles's position in Paris as husband of a pretty and fashionable woman was
rather a trying one.   With a father whose
sparkling wit made him everywhere take
a leading part in society, he was thrown
into the shade, and reduced to a secondary
position, which, however, his modesty would
not have objected to had he not felt that
it lowered him in his wife's estimation.

When he married, it was without any feeling
of love for Hélène, whom he had hardly
seen, but he soon felt a tender and almost
paternal affection for her. He had allowed
her the greatest freedom at Bel Œil, at
the same time seeking to develop in her a
taste for serious occupations hitherto rather
checked by her intense love of pleasure. He
was beginning to succeed, but these three
winters in Paris almost annulled his efforts,
or at least greatly compromised their success.
Hélène was too young to understand and
appreciate her husband's superior intelligence
and high character.

However, a long - desired event brought
the married pair nearer to each other for
a while. On the 8th of December 1786
Hélène gave birth to a little girl, who received
the name of Sidonie. This was a great joy
to Prince Charles, and he easily obtained
Hélène's consent to go to Bel Œil in the
early spring, instead of returning to Paris.
She consented the more willingly that her

father-in-law had left Paris for the Russian
Court, whither he had been summoned by
an invitation from the Empress Catherine.

Before starting the Prince had had ample
time to construct the bower of roses he had
promised for Charles's children, and as early
as the month of March a handsome Brabant
nurse, carrying a pink and white baby, might
be seen in the gardens of Bel Œil. Everything seemed to promise a happy summer,
and in spite of the somewhat unrestricted
authority exercised over the nurse and
baby by the Dowager-Princess, which was a
source of annoyance to the young mother,
harmony and peace prevailed at Bel Œil.

All of a sudden, in the middle of the
summer (1787), a serious insurrection broke
out in Flanders. It had been secretly
brewing for some time past. Joseph II. had
the mania of meddling in everything; he
generally had the best intentions, but, cleverer
in theory than in practice, he often neglected to ascertain whether a system useful

in itself might not become dangerous if applied without any previous preparation. The
reforms he tried to introduce into Flanders
are a striking example of this sort of mistake.

The Flemish people, who had long been
under the dominion of Spain, were bigoted
in their religion, and as deeply attached to
their ancient political privileges as they were
to those of the Church. After the death of
Marie-Thérèse, Joseph II. began by abolish-
ing certain processions, pilgrimages, and a
number of confraternities. These customs
and institutions, which were certainly useless
and far too numerous, were closely interwoven
with the habits of the people, and their aboli-
tion was a source of great offence. The
clergy were not less offended at the decree
that suppressed the Bollandists, numerous
convents and abbeys, and all the diocesan
seminaries.

Finally the Emperor, still animated with
the most liberal intentions, thought that "it
was his charitable duty to extend towards

Protestants the effects of that civil tolerance
which, without inquiring into 'a' man's belief,
considers only his capacity as citizen." He
accordingly granted them a civil existence—
a privilege which till then had been refused
to them.

The Bishops loudly protested against
these measures, and were severely re-
primanded.   Not content with attacking the
privileges of the Church, Joseph II. upset the
judicial organisation of the country, and in a
way suppressed the nationality of the Netherlands, which were declared to be an Austrian
province, divided into nine circles, governed
by an *intendant* and Austrian commissioners,
solely dependent on the Viennese Court.   This
was trampling underfoot the "*Joyeuse Entrée*"
(Joyous Entry), that grand charta of the
privileges of Brabant and the other Flemish
States.[1]

---

[1] Amongst others, the privileges of Hainault were most curious.
We find there the formula of the ancient oath which the Emperor
took at his inauguration as Comte de Hainault.

The irritation was at its height, for Joseph had by his various reforms succeeded in alienating every class of his subjects.

A barrister of Brussels, Van der Noot, published an extremely violent manifesto, demonstrating the illegality of the innovations introduced by Joseph II. This libel was approved of by the States,[1] but the author, in danger of being arrested by the Government, fled to England. It was at the very moment when the revolution was being fomented that the de Ligne family, alarmed at the agitation going on in Belgium, hastened to join Prince Charles at Vienna, whither he had been summoned by Marshal Lascy. An army, destined to fight the Turks in the ensuing spring, was already being organised by the Emperor's secret orders. The Princesses de Ligne reached Vienna at the end of the

---

[1] The States of Hainault took an active part in the rebellion, and refused in October 1788 to vote the subsidies demanded by the Emperor. They had been mortally offended when an Austrian Commissioner superseded their former governor and grand bailiff, the Prince of Aremberg.

summer.   Hélène had made a short stay there at the time of her marriage, and had not retained an agreeable recollection of the place.   The Viennese manners and customs differed too much from the French to suit her taste.   She would infinitely have preferred spending the winter in her hotel at Paris ; but her husband's duties detaining him in Vienna, she dared not make the request.

The Emperor of Germany's Court did not display the brilliant aspect which might have been expected from the most important European power.[1]   The simple architecture of his palace conveyed no idea of a sovereign's residence.   A detachment of the

---

[1] The House of Lorraine had greatly contributed to banish the severe etiquette which till then prevailed at the Viennese Court.

Francis the First, father of Marie-Antoinette, invited to his table the principal Crown officials, and allowed the most perfect freedom. Marie-Thérèse admitted to her intimacy most of the ladies of her Court ; she even during the summer paid frequent visits to several of them. She might be seen, knitting and walking in the gardens, or reading in an arbour, unattended by any of her ladies.   Marie-Antoinette had therefore from her infancy been accustomed to those habits of ease and familiarity which she carried to France, and which caused her to be so severely censured.

Viennese garrison mounted guard, and a few *trabans* posted at the inner doors superintended the management and good order of the interior.   Joseph II.'s household was very economically conducted.   He had, however, grand Crown officials, such as grand-master, lord high chamberlain, grand-equerry, etc. But they only fulfilled their duties on gala days.   In spite of the plainness and simplicity of the Viennese Court, the personages who composed it were of very high standing; there were many reigning princes, brothers of kings or electors, in the service of the Emperor, and a crowd of great nobles, such as the Princes de Ligne, d'Aremberg, de Lichtenstein, Esterhazi, Colorado, Palfy,[1] and others, who by their rank and future were almost equal to their sovereign.   When he chose, the Emperor "knew how to impart to this Court, which usually had the appearance of a convent or a barrack, all the pomp

---

[1] The Princesse Euphémie de Ligne married, 11th September 1798, Jean-Baptiste Gabriel, the eldest son of the Comte de Palfy.

and dignity worthy of the palace of Marie-
Thérèse.

Hélène witnessed for the first time
the New Year's festivities at Vienna. On
that day most of the Hungarian magnates [1]
came to Court in their elegant costumes,
decked out with their handsomest jewels ; the
Prince Esterhazi, among others, was mounted
on a richly caparisoned horse whose saddle-
cloth was studded with diamonds. The
Prince's costume was as rich as his horse's
trappings. " I could not look at him,"
Hélène says; "he dazzled me." The Emperor
Joseph, so simple in private life, wore a full-
dress uniform embroidered with gold, and his
coat, his orders, and his hat glittered with
eighteen hundred thousand livres [2] worth of

---

[1] The guard of Hungarian nobles only escorted the Emperor on
great state occasions. It was supported by the Hungarian States,
who took great pride in the beauty of the horses and splendour of
the uniforms.

The Polish guard, created after the first Polish division (1772),
was composed of young noblemen, and vied in brilliancy with the
Hungarian guard.

[2] Seventy-two thousand pounds.

diamonds; the buttons, the fastenings, the epaulets, the braid, and the button of his hat were one mass of diamonds. On that day the Court servants and those of the nobility wore a livery of silk embroidered with gold and silver.

The Prince de Ligne has left an interesting portrait of Joseph II., with whom he had been on terms of the closest intimacy. A year before the commencement of the Emperor's reign, Lord Malmesbury asked the Prince de Ligne what he thought of him. "As a man," replied the Prince, "he possesses great merit and talent; as Prince he will always be tortured by ambitions which he will be unable to satisfy; his reign will be a sort of perpetual and vain longing to sneeze."

The Emperor Joseph was fond of the society of amiable and distinguished women, but no love intrigue ever arose in his intimate circle. The Princesse Kinsky, born a Hohenzollern, and her sister, the Princesse Clary,[1] were both conspicuous at Court. The first

---

[1] Mother-in-law of the Princesse Christine de Ligne.

was simple and affable, had much learning, possessed a sound judgment, and was passionately fond of reading and conversation. The second, modest, gentle, and gracious, was a better listener than her sister, and her pliant disposition imparted great charm and ease to her society. The Emperor had given the Princesse Kinsky a very fine apartment in his palace of the Haut Belvédère.[1] It was there that the choicest Viennese society, both of men and women, would meet every Thursday. As a great favour Hélène was admitted to this circle, and she has traced a few portraits of these ladies—amongst others, that of the Princesse Charles de Lichtenstein, born Princesse d'Œttingen, who was the darling of the Belvédère society. She was exquisitely beautiful, and wrote marvellously well. Her letters, nearly all written in French, overflowed with wit; she expressed herself with elegance ; and her firm and reliable character,

---

[1] A small palace built by Prince Eugène in one of the suburbs of Vienna.

her amiable and cultivated mind, so won the heart of the Prince de Ligne that she became his favourite sister-in-law.

The Comtesse Ernest de Kaunitz,[1] sister of the Princesse Charles, was plain, but witty and lively. She would often provoke a discussion, for she loved an argument, and excelled in the vivacity and archness of her repartee. The Princesse François de Lichtenstein, born Steinberg, completed the little circle. Second sister-in-law of the Prince de Ligne, she pleased him less than the first ; she had an exalted idea of her rank and name, and of the consideration that was due to her. Serious and dignified, but at the same time kind and benevolent, she was constantly occupied with charitable works, and it was difficult to escape the lottery tickets, concerts, and collections for the poor she imposed upon every one.

---

[1] Daughter-in-law of the famous Prince de Kaunitz, Chancellor of the Empire under Marie-Thérèse. He had retained office under Joseph, and was one of the most influential persons at Court.

The only stranger admitted into this society was the Duc de Braganza. The Marshal de Lascy, the Prince de Kaunitz, the Prince de Ligne, and several other gentlemen of the Court frequently came, and the Emperor Joseph never missed a Thursday at the Belvédère.

In his youth Joseph II. did not give much promise of amiability, but he changed entirely when he became Emperor. His travels, his campaigns, the society of distinguished women, had formed his character and cured him of a shyness engendered by the extreme severity of his education.

The greatest freedom existed in the Belvédère circle ; the Emperor laid aside his rank and allowed the ladies to speak with a frankness that sometimes exceeded the bounds of respect.

" The things I have heard said to Joseph by the ladies of his society are simply inconceivable," writes the Prince de Ligne. " One of them said, referring to the execution of a

robber who had been hanged by his orders
that day : ‘ How could your Majesty condemn
him after your robbery of Poland ?’

“ It was at the moment of the first division of that country.

“‘ My mother, who enjoys all your confidence, ladies,’ he replied, ‘and who goes to
Mass as often as you do, has long ago made
up her mind on that question.   I am only her
first subject.’ ”

The Emperor was fond of receiving confidences, and was safe and discreet, though he
was fond of meddling.   His manners were
agreeable, he had some brilliancy of conversation, a great deal of natural wit, and was a
pleasant narrator.   The following is an anec-
dote he was fond of repeating.   When Marie-
Thérèse was so closely pursued by her enemies
that hardly a town was left to her in Germany,
not knowing where to go for her confinement,
she retired to Presburg and assembled the
States.   She was young and handsome, with a
dazzling complexion, and appeared before the

Hungarian *paladins* clad in a long mourning garment, which set off the radiancy of her beauty; her son, two or three years of age, was clasped in her arms. " I confide him to you," she said, presenting the child, who began to cry. The Emperor, in telling this story, always added that his mother, who knew the way to produce an effect, gave him a sly pinch as she presented him to the Hungarians ; touched by the cries of the child, who seemed to implore their compassion, " my bearded heroes drew their swords, and swore on their Turkish blades to defend both mother and son to the last drop of their blood."[1]

The little group that met at the Belvédère did not represent the only society in Vienna ; many other houses threw open their doors. The Princesse Lubomirska,[2] com-

---

[1] Fragments of the Prince de Ligne's *Unedited Memoirs*, published in the *Revue Nouvelle*, 1840, and by Albert Lacroix at Brussels.

[2] The Princesse Lubomirska was a cousin of the King Stanislaus-Augustus. He frequently mentions her in his correspondence with Madame Geoffrin under the name of Aspasia. She was a

monly called the Princesse Maréchale, held
some of the most brilliant receptions. Her
original and ready wit, and the piquancy of
her manner, imparted a certain liveliness to
the character of her " salon." She forebade
all talk of war or politics at her house. " No
politics," she said, " in the drawing-room,
where the men are more women than we
are."

A great many balls were given in Vienna,
and they were always very animated, for the
Viennese were passionately fond of dancing.
They waltzed so furiously and with such
rapidity that at first Hélène, though a beautiful dancer, was made quite giddy by the
pace. She, however, soon became accustomed, like others, never to rest for a moment
as long as the waltz lasted.

The balls of the Princesse Lubomirska were
delightful ; they always began and ended with

Czartoryiska by birth, and alternately resided at Vienna, Warsaw,
and at her magnificent estate of Lancut. A large part of the
Princess's lands was situated in Austrian Galicia.

a polonaise, a kind of measured march, interrupted at intervals by a graceful *balancé* or
swinging movement. "When the elderly
people wish to join in the dance they ask for
a polonaise," says the Prince de Ligne, "and
then the good people perform the figures,
and move round with a contented smile on
their faces, as they recollect the good old
times, and the way they used to smile. The
young people are entirely taken up with the
present, of which they do not care to lose a
moment." This dance displayed to advantage the elegance and grace of the figure.
Hélène excelled in it, and took a patriotic
pride in carrying off the palm.

The Princesse Charles was passionately
fond of music, and had a box at the Court
theatre. *Don Juan* had just been given with
great success at Prague, in honour of the
visit of the Duchess of Tuscany, the wife of
Leopold. Mozart had in person directed the
rehearsals. The Emperor Joseph, about to
leave for the army, pressed Mozart to return

to Vienna to get up the opera there at once. The rehearsals were rapidly got through, and the representation was given before a large audience. Hélène was present, and all the Viennese nobility witnessed the performance. *Don Juan* was admirably sung, but the public, with few exceptions, of which Hélène was one, remained cold throughout. The Emperor, who thought the music admirable, was vexed at the indifference of the audience.

"It is a divine work," he said to Mozart, whom he had summoned to his box, " but it is not the sort of thing for my Viennese!"

"We must give them time to appreciate it," modestly replied the author. "It suited the Prague people better; but I composed it only for myself and my friends."

On leaving the theatre some of the spectators went to the house of the Comtesse de Thun, and they were warmly discussing the new work when Haydn entered. Every one was of a different opinion, and though admitting for the most part that the music bore the impress of genius, all declared that in some parts it was obscure and incomprehensible. Haydn was chosen as judge. " I am not in a position to decide in such a learned dispute," said he with malicious humility ; " all I know is that Mozart is the greatest musician living."

The concerts at Vienna were numerous and most magnificent. The Emperor had a passion for instrumental music. Mozart and Haydn's[1] symphonies were played with rare perfection by an excellent orchestra, led by Salieri.[2] It was likewise in the spring of 1787 that the *Seven Words* were given for the first time—an oratorio which is looked upon as Haydn's masterpiece.

It is evident that Hélène might have spent

---

[1] Mozart was appointed to the Emperor's chapel in 1780. Joseph II. was very fond of him, and although his salary was very small, he always refused the advantageous offers made by other sovereigns, among others the King of Prussia. Haydn was also attached to the Emperor's chapel.

[2] Salieri, chapel-master and music-director to the Emperor at Vienna.

a most agreeable winter in Vienna, but she
did not like Viennese society. A Parisian
at heart, she felt there entirely out of her
element. Her husband, on the other hand,
who had known all the families about Court
from childhood, was infinitely more at home
in Vienna than in Paris. He was on the most
intimate terms with all the young married
women who were friends of his sisters. One
of them in particular treated him with the
affectionate familiarity of an old playfellow ;
this was the Comtesse Kinsky, born a
Dietrichstein, and daughter-in-law to the
Princess presiding at the Belvédère. It
would have been difficult to meet with a
more fascinating woman, and her romantic
story added greatly to her charm. Comte
Kinsky's parents and her own had agreed on
a marriage between their children without
consulting them on the subject. The young
Count was garrisoned in a small Hungarian
town, and only arrived in time for the
marriage ceremony. Immediately afterwards

he conducted his young wife home, kissed her hand, and said : " Madame, we have obeyed our parents ; and I must confess it is with regret that I leave you ; but my affections have long been engaged to a woman without whom I cannot live, and to whom I must now return." A post-chaise was at the door of the church ; the Count drove off and never returned. Comtesse Kinsky was therefore neither maid, wife, nor widow, and the dangers of this peculiar position were enhanced by her extreme beauty, which it would have been difficult to outrival. She united to her external charms a cultivated mind and an excellent heart. Hélène often met her at the Comtesse de Thun's, who was an intimate friend of the de Lignes, and whose house was their habitual rendezvous.

Comte François de Dietrichstein,[1] Madame

[1] The Comte François-Joseph de Dietrichstein, born 28th April 1767, was private counsellor and chamberlain to the Austrian Emperor. He filled the post of Major-General in the Engineers during the first wars against the French republic, and it was he who n 1800 concluded with Moreau the armistice of Parsdorf.

de Kinsky's brother, was a great friend of Prince Charles, with whom he had been brought up. The peculiar position of the Countess rendered this intimacy very hazardous, and Prince Charles's tender affection for her partook very much of the nature of love. With a woman's quick instinct, Hélène divined between her husband and the beautiful Countess a secret tie, the nature of which she could not make out, the strictest propriety being observed on both sides. We must admit that, in spite of little Sidonie's birth, which for a moment drew the pair more closely together, they were becoming very indifferent towards each other. The Prince had not forgotten the contemptuous manner with which his wife had treated him in Paris, and he was not sorry to show her that in Vienna he played quite a different part. In short, neither one nor the other had made a love match. Social conventions and a similarity of tastes had conduced to a certain degree of friendship ; but would that suffice to guard either against any warmer sentiment that might intervene ?

And so the winter passed. The revolution in Flanders had assumed alarming proportions, and there could be no question of returning to Bel Œil. Prince Charles, who had rejoined his regiment, served under General de Lascy's orders, and had left Vienna for some time. No sooner had he taken his departure than Hélène wrote to ask his permission to join her uncle at Warsaw, where the Diet was about to meet. Some important business with the Prince-Bishop served as a pretext for the journey. The authorisation was easily granted, on condition that she should leave little Sidonie under the care of her grandmother ; and Hélène left Vienna in September 1788.

IX

IN the autumn of the year 1786 the Prince de Ligne received an invitation from the Czarina, asking him to join her at St. Petersburg, and accompany her in a journey she was about to undertake in the Crimea. This invitation was secretly intended to prepare an interview that was to take place at Kherson between Catherine and Joseph II. Turkey had ceded the Crimea and Kouban to Russia in January 1784. These acquisitions had only aggravated Catherine's thirst for further conquest. She already betrayed her ambition

in the smallest details : one of her grandsons
had been named Alexander, and the other
Constantine ; the Crimea was now again
called Tauris ; but her ambitious designs did
not end there. The Empress received the
Prince de Ligne as if he had only left her
the day before, informed him of her plans,
and at the end of December sent him back
to Joseph with the itinerary of her journey
and the result of his secret mission.

Under the pretext of visiting her new dominions the Czarina undertook on the 15th of
January 1787 a journey through the southern
provinces of her empire. She was accompanied by her favourite, Count Momonoff, and
by the ambassadors of France, Austria, and
England, and by the Prince de Ligne, who
met her at Kief. " I occupied," he says, " the
position of a diplomatic jockey."

She was also accompanied by a considerable number of princes and Russian lords.
Her flotilla consisted of eighty-four ships,
manned by three thousand seamen.

The King, Stanislaus-Augustus, awaited
the Czarina at Kanew. She slowly descended
the Borysthenes in a galley as magnificent as
that of Cleopatra. The Prince de Ligne left
the flotilla in a small Zaporavian canoe to
announce Catherine's arrival to the King. An
hour later the great lords of the empire came
to fetch him in a gunboat brilliantly decorated.
Whilst stepping on board he said, with the
inexpressible charm of manner and pleasant
tone of voice so peculiar to him : "Gentlemen, the King of Poland has requested me to
commend to you Comte Poniatowski." The
dinner was very gay, and while the King's
health was drunk, three salutes were fired by
the artillery of the whole fleet. Afterwards
the King gave a supper to all the nobles of
his retinue. The fleet had cast anchor before
the palace improvised for him ; no sooner
had night closed in than a general conflagra-
tion on the neighbouring shores of the Borysthenes simulated an eruption of Vesuvius,
lighting up the valleys, the mountains, and

the river in a most glorious manner. The glare of the fires lit up the fantastic display of the brilliant squadrons of Polish cavalry. Stanislaus had spent three months and three millions in order to see the Czarina for three hours. She had loved him, but, long ago, this love had been replaced by others; and now she slowly and cruelly tore from him the shreds of the kingdom she had formerly bestowed. They separated with all the appearance of friendliness, but during their short meeting the King had had time to perceive that there was no hope of reviving the past.

This was the last interview that took place between Catherine and Stanislaus. Eight years later she dethroned him with her own hands.

The Emperor Joseph met the Czarina at Kherson, and they continued together on their travels, which resembled those of a fairy tale. "I still fancy I am dreaming," says the Prince de Ligne, "when I recall that

journey, in an enormous coach large enough
for six people, quite a triumphal chariot in
fact, studded all over with precious stones,
and drawn by sixteen horses of the Tartar
race.   How, as I sat between two persons, on
whose shoulders I would sink at times, overcome by the heat, I would be startled by
such snatches of conversation as these :—

  " ' I have thirty millions of subjects, I am
told, counting only the males.'

  " ' And I, twenty-two,' replied the other,
' counting all.'

  " They made imaginary conquests of towns
and provinces, as if that were nothing at all,
whilst I kept on saying : ' Your Majesties will
reap nothing but worry and misery,' to which
the Emperor would reply, addressing himself to the Empress : ' Madame, we treat him
too well ; he has no respect for us.   Did you
know, Madame, that he had been in love with
one of my father's mistresses, and at the time
of my first successes in society he outwitted
me in the affections of a marchioness who

was an object of adoration to both of us, and as beautiful as an angel?'"

During the journey the Empress had made a gift of the site of Iphigenia's rock to the Prince de Ligne. All those who possessed land in the Crimea, such as the Mourzas, took the oath of fidelity to Catherine, and the Prince de Ligne followed suit. The Emperor came up to him, and taking hold of his order of the Golden Fleece, said: "You are the first one of this order who has sworn allegiance together with the long-bearded lords."

"Sire," said de Ligne, with a malicious air, "it is better both for your Majesty and myself that I should take it with the Tartar lords than with those of Flanders."

The Emperor had just heard of the rebellion in that country, of which we shall speak later on.

After their return from this fairy-like journey the war against the Turks was decided, and the Austro-Russian alliance concluded.

Preparations for war were being quietly carried on when, all at once, Turkey assumed the offensive by arresting the Russian ambassador, M. de Bulgakoff, and confining him in the Castle of the Sept Tours (Seven Towers). On the 18th of August 1787 Catherine declared war.

The Empress thoroughly relied on the alliance she had just concluded with Joseph II.; nevertheless she inquired of the Prince de Ligne :—

"What do you think the Emperor will do ?"

"Have you any doubt, Madame ? He will convey to you his good intentions, perhaps even his best wishes ; and as neither will cost him anything, I am sure his first letter will be full of them."

The Prince was mistaken ; the Emperor was ready to appear on the field with a hundred thousand men,[1] and had just appointed the Prince General-Commander-in-

---

[1] On 9th February 1788 Austria, in fulfilment of her alliance with Russia, declared war with Turkey.

chief (feldzeugmeister) of all the infantry. Unfortunately the letter bringing this news crossed one the Prince had written to the Emperor asking his permission to serve as a general in the Russian army, and at the same time offering to keep His Majesty well informed of the Russian plans of campaign and military operations. The Emperor granted this request.

The Prince began preparing for his departure in October 1787. "I received," he says, "from the Emperor a letter concerning his ally that showed both his kindness and genius; I made a summary of it that served as a plan of campaign, for none had as yet been conceived at Saint Petersburg. They had no idea by what end to begin."

Before starting to join Potemkin[1] the

---

[1] Potemkin (Grégoire Alexandrowitch), Russian Field-Marshal, and the most renowned favourite of Catherine II. He was born in September 1736, in the suburbs of Smolensk, and died on 16th October 1791

It is said that during the famous journey in Tauris he ordered theatrical scenery to be constructed at intervals on the road along which the Empress was expected to pass. This scenery re-

Prince wished to give a ball to the prettiest women at Court, according to their request, but was unable to do so, as the war operations were already far advanced. " The army," he was told, "may perhaps be already under the walls of Oczakoff; five thousand Turks have been killed by Souvaroff at Kinburn. The Turkish fleet is retiring; start at once."

He left on the 1st of November 1787. "Good heavens!" he writes, "what weather! what roads! what a winter! what head-quarters! By nature I am confiding, and always believe I am loved. I thought the Prince, judging by his own words, would

presented in the distance villages, towns, and cities, and he organised troops of supernumerary actors, who simulated the rural population peacefully pursuing their avocations. Although he was invested with offices and dignities more profitable one than the other, he helped himself to the State monies, and accepted bribes from foreign powers. Joseph II. and Frederick the Great loaded him with presents and pensions, and in consequence of their rivalry with regard to the Russian alliance, the first created him Prince of the Holy Roman Empire, and the second offered to assist him in obtaining for himself the Duchy of Courland. He had no talent as a general in command, but was fortunate in having under him good officers, who were able to carry on the war operations against the Turks.

be delighted to see me. I only observed six months later the embarrassed manner. in which he received me on the day of my arrival. I threw myself into his arms and said :—

"'When shall we take Oczakoff?'

"'Who knows!' he said; 'the garrison numbers eighteen thousand men; I have not as many in the whole of my army. I am short of everything, and the most unhappy of mortals, unless God helps me.'

"'What!' I replied, 'the story of Kinburn, the departure of the fleet, has all that been of no use? I have travelled day and night, for they told me you had already begun the siege!'

"'Alas,' he answered, 'God grant that the Tartars do not get here, and lay waste the whole country with fire and sword. God has saved me (I shall never forget it). He allowed me to collect behind the banks of the Bog what remained of the troops. It is a miracle that I have retained till now as much of the country as I have.'

"'Where are the Tartars?' said I.

"'Everywhere,' he replied, 'and among them is a séraskier,[1] with a large number of Turks, near Ackermann, twelve thousand men in Bender, the Dniester is guarded, and there are six thousand men in Choczim.'"

There was not a word of truth in all this. Five months were spent in a state of inactivity which would have been inexplicable had it not been intentional. The Prince de Ligne was not long in perceiving that this was the case, and punctually warned the Emperor of Austria.

During the long days of *far niente* the Prince amused himself by scribbling down his thoughts on little squares of paper, which, though he appeared to attach no importance to them, he took care to preserve. They were well worth keeping, to judge by the following :—

"Europe is in such a perfect mess at the

---

[1] Seraskier, general-in-chief in the Turkish army.

present moment that I think it a good time
to reflect on the position of affairs.   France
writes, but, unfortunately, the Empire reads.
The soldiers of the Bishop of Liege are
at open war with the bankers of Spa.
The Netherlands have risen against their
sovereign without knowing why.   Soon, no
doubt, people will kill one another in the
hope of gaining more freedom and happiness.
Austria, exposed to dangers at home, timidly
threatens both friend and foe, and is unable
to distinguish one from the other.   England,
who is never entirely of the same opinion,
has a majority in favour of Prussia, who has
already fired a few shots in Holland!   Proud
Spain, who formerly owned the invincible
fleet, gets anxious as soon as a single
English vessel leaves port.   Italy fears the
lazzaroni and the free-thinkers.   Denmark
watches Sweden, and Sweden watches
Russia.   The Tartars, the Georgians, the
Imarets, the Abyssinians, the Circassians, kill
the Russians.   The journey to the Crimea

alarms and irritates the Sultan. The Egyptian and Scutari bashaws are warring with the Turks, who, from two other sides, at a thousand leagues' distance, are at the same time attacking the two most powerful and important empires that exist. We are called to arms, and I join the fray. Without ceasing to be a spectator, I become an actor in the play. In my opinion all that is taking place around me is nothing more than a kick in an anthill. Are we anything better ourselves, poor mortals that we are?"

During this time the corps under Marshal Lascy[1] had opened the campaign; the Emperor commanded in person, and Prince Charles, who had not accompanied his father to Russia, served as major in the engineers.

---

[1] Joseph-François-Maurice,Comte de Lascy,born at St. Petersburg on 21st October 1725, and educated at Vienna. He was colonel when the Seven Years War broke out. The services he rendered ensured him rapid promotion; he distinguished himself during the campaign of 1778, and in 1788, as field-marshal, conducted the war against the Turks. He died at Vienna on 4th November 1801.

The Prince soon distinguished himself at the siege of Sabacz, where he superintended the opening of the trenches, and directed the batteries which attacked the fort.

On the day of the assault, by means of a plank, he crossed the wide deep moats which protected the approaches of the fortress; he was the first to dash forward and scale the wall, and once on the top of the ramparts, in spite of the efforts of the Turks, he held out his hand to the soldiers who had followed him, helped them up, and was the first to enter the town. The Emperor, who witnessed this brilliant exploit, conferred on the Prince the rank of Colonel, and decorated him with the order of Marie-Thérèse, without holding a chapter of the order—an honour which was entirely without precedent. It so happened that the garrison of Belgrade was carrying on such a heavy cannonading during the ceremony that the Emperor Joseph, addressing the Prince, said: " Even the Turks are taking part in your initiation, and celebrating your valour and my justice."

The Emperor himself announced to the Prince de Ligne his son's brilliant conduct: the pride and emotion of the father can only be described in his own words. He writes to the Comte de Ségur :—

8th May 1788.

"Ah! my friend, let me weep awhile; and read the following!

" ' THE EMPEROR JOSEPH TO THE PRINCE DE LIGNE.

" ' KILENACK, 25*th April* 1788.

" ' We have just taken Sabacz :[1] our loss was small. The feldzeugmeister, Rouvroy,[2] a brave man, as you know, received a slight wound in the chest, which does not prevent

---

[1] A fortified town in Servia, situated on the Save; 4000 inhabitants.

[2] Theodore, Baron de Rouvroy, born at Luxembourg in 1727. He entered the Austrian service in 1753, and in 1765 received the cross of commander of the order of Marie-Thérèse. He died 31st September 1789. He was one of the most distinguished artillery generals in the Austrian army.

him from dressing himself or going out.
Prince Poniatowski was shot in the thigh,
and though the bone is not injured the wound
is somewhat serious.   But I must, my dear
Prince, inform you of something else, which
will please you all the more that in it you
will recognise the spirit of your race; it is
that your son Charles contributed for the
most part to the success of this enterprise,
by the infinite pains that he took in marking
out the trenches for the batteries, and he was
the first to scale the parapet and help up the
rest.   So I have named him Lieutenant-
Colonel, and have conferred on him the
order of Marie-Thérèse.   It is a real pleasure to me to send you this intelligence, as
I am aware of the satisfaction it will give
you, knowing, as I do, your patriotism and
your affection for your son.

"'I leave to-morrow for Semlin.

"'JOSEPH.'

"What modesty!   The Emperor does not

mention himself, though he was in the midst of the firing. And how graciously and kindly expressed is the account he sends me. On reading it over again I burst into tears."

8th May (*continued from the above*).

" The messenger saw the Emperor himself firing musket shots with hearty goodwill into the suburbs of Sabacz; and Marshal de Lascy tear up some palings to point a cannon, which should protect my Charles by attacking a turret from which a continual fire was being directed against him. The Marshal would, I believe, have done it for any other, but it had the appearance of personal and almost paternal kindness.

" The Marshal being rather exhausted, the Emperor fetched a barrel and made him sit down, while he himself stood surrounded by his generals, thus paying him a kind of homage.

" Here is a letter from Charles himself :—

" ' We have taken Sabacz. I have the

cross. You may be sure, papa, that I thought of you on going up the first to the assault.—Your submissive and respectful son,

"'CHARLES.'

"Could there be anything more touching! Would I had been there to give him a hand! I can see that I have his esteem by the words, *I thought of you*, but I should have deserved it still better. I feel too much affected to write more. I embrace you, my dear Count."

But it is with his son that the Prince gives himself up to all the intensity of his feelings.

FROM POTEMKIN'S HEADQUARTERS AT
ELISABETHGOROD.

12*th May* 1788.

"What can I tell you, my dear Charles, that you do not already know of my feelings on receiving from His Majesty a letter so full of kindness and graciousness? This letter is worth more to you than any parchments containing titles, diplomas, or patents—mere food for rats. It contains such touching words for us both that, though I am getting rather old to cry, it is impossible for me to refrain from doing so whenever I read over that paragraph. All the Circassian generals and officers, the Zaporogues, Tartars, Cabardians,[1] Germans, Russians, Cossacks, etc.,—all came to me in crowds, to congratulate me with a warmth I can never forget.

" The father and most tender friend of my Charles are assuredly deeply touched at the honour you have won, and which surpasses anything I have ever done in my life. But the General de Ligne has suffered abominably.

" Imagine, my boy, what a delightful moment for both of us had I been the first to accept your aid in clambering up that parapet, where you arrived before any one else !

" Good heavens, what a fool one is at a distance ! I, who at Hühnerwasser would

---

[1] Inhabitants of Cabardia, a country situated on the northern slopes of the Caucasus, and which, at that time, was not yet under Russian dominion.

have calmly seen you shot through the arm—
I am as nervous as any woman,—a condition
which is not far removed from that of
minister.[1]   However, I have agreed with
some regiments of light horse to make a
good slashing charge.   I have never done
anything of the kind, except at the head of
ten Uhlans against five or six drunken
Prussian hussars.   You will admit that it
was not the most memorable action of this
century.   I cannot shut myself up in those
squares, as in a box, where one opens a door
to come in or go out.

"One can always manage to command if
one chooses on the day of battle, so that I am
perfectly certain, though I have not an army,
that nothing will happen where I am but what
I choose ; I have already learnt all that is
necessary, and am beginning to understand
Russian.   Do you think now, my Charles,
that I was right in always wishing you to be

---

[1] The Prince was both General-in-Chief without an army corps
and Minister-plenipotentiary *in partibus.*

an engineer ?   You have now shown genius,[1]
as I knew you would.   But are you sure you
are not slightly wounded, though you do not
say so ?

"Do not let any of His Majesty's mes-
sengers come to me without sending me a
letter.   A thousand messages to my comrade
Rouvroy, whose fate and wound I envy.
Poor Poniatowski![2] I tremble lest he should
follow in his father's footsteps.   He has
already the same courage, the same military
intelligence, personal devotion to His Majesty,
generosity, etc., but I trust he will not have
the same fate.   Embrace him for me."

The news of the taking of Sabacz had

---

[1] A play upon words; "genius" and "engineer" in French
being expressed by the same word, *génie.*

[2] Prince Joseph Poniatowski was at that time lieutenant-colonel
and aide-de-camp to the Emperor of Austria.   He entered the Polish
army as general in 1789.   He had command of the army at Warsaw
in 1809.   The Emperor Napoleon made him a Marshal of France.
At Sabacz the Turks took him for the Emperor Joseph, as he
wore the same uniform—a green coat with red facings, and a
brilliant decoration.   He was killed by a shot while crossing the
Elster on 19th October 1813.

made a welcome break in the weary existence the Prince's father was leading; but Potemkin's apathy made him relapse into bad
humour and impatience. He tried in vain to
sting his pride by making constant allusions
to the storming of Sabacz, but he had rightly
guessed "that, either out of policy, ill-will,
or incapacity, the marshals were resolved,
even before the campaign was begun, on
doing nothing."

At last, wearied by this determined
inaction, he wrote to Prince Potemkin that
he should leave the next day for Marshal
Romanzoff's[1] camp in Ukrania.

"At last," writes the Prince, "I have left
those filthy entrenchments which, in virtue

---

[1] Romanzoff (Pierre Alexandrowitch), born in 1725, was one of
the most celebrated Russian generals. He defeated Frederick the
Second at the battle of Kunersdorf. Appointed Commander-in-
Chief of the Russian army in 1770 during the war against the
Turks, he obtained several brilliant successes, and was named
field-marshal. He was so dissatisfied at sharing the command with
Potemkin in 1787 that he did not continue the campaign, and
resigned his post. This motive may also explain his inaction. He
died on 17th December 1796.

of a few projecting angles, are supposed to represent a fort; eight days more and I should have died of it.   Potemkin nearly drove me mad.   Sometimes on good terms, sometimes on bad, at daggers drawn or prime favourite, speaking or not speaking, but sitting up sometimes till six in the morning to induce him at least to say one word sensible enough to report,—I could no longer endure the whims of such a spoilt child."

Wearied to death by this horrible inaction, the Prince went to see why Marshal Romanzoff was no better employed than Potemkin.

Romanzoff, as amiable as Potemkin was the reverse, loaded the Prince with promises and attentions, all equally false.   At the end of a few days Ligne was fully convinced that the two Commanders-in-Chief of the Russian army were agreed on one point— "to play a trick on the Emperor Joseph, and only begin the campaign in July, by which time the whole of the Turkish forces would have been directed against the

Austrians." The Prince de Ligne redoubled his efforts to stir up Potemkin. He wrote to the Austrian ambassador at St. Petersburg, and to the Comte de Ségur, urging them to inform the Empress of the situation ; but though himself in such favour at Court he never once wrote to Catherine. She knew the motive of his silence, and was irritated at it ; but she would not complain, in case that, in a fit of frankness, the Prince should say too much. "If I had chosen," he says, "to write only once in praise of Prince Potemkin and his operations,[1] I should have received showers of presents in diamonds and serfs. Catherine would have been very well pleased

---

[1] The Prince de Ligne relates that Prince Potemkin had only one idea—that of forming a regiment of Jews, to be called Israelowsky. "We already had a squadron whom I delighted in ; for their long beards, which reached to their knees, on account of their short stirrups, and the fear they were in on horseback, gave them the appearance of monkeys. The anxiety they felt could be read in their eyes, and the long pikes they carried in a most comical manner made them look as if they were trying to mimic the Cossacks. I do not know what cursed *Pope* (Russian priest) persuaded our Marshal that a corps of Jews was contrary to the Holy Scriptures."

if I had deceived her ; it would have been more convenient for her to believe that all was going on well."

In spite of his anger against the Russian Marshals the Prince de Ligne, who was a connoisseur, sincerely admired the Muscovite nation and soldiery.

" I see that the Russians," he writes to the Comte de Ségur, "learn the liberal arts in the same way that *le médecin malgré lui* (the doctor in spite of himself) took his degree. They are foot-soldiers, sailors, sportsmen, priests, dragoons, musicians, engineers, actors, cuirassiers, painters and surgeons. I see the Russians sing and dance in the trenches, though they are never relieved, and remain in the midst of shot and shell, of snow or mud, clever, clean, attentive, respectful, obedient, trying to forestall their orders by divining them in the eyes of their officers."

The greatest pleasure the General de Ligne had was to write and receive news of absent friends. His letters are so wonderfully graphic, the slightest detail is invested with so much charm, that one is never tired of reading them. Those he wrote to his son Charles are a perfect diary of his life.

FROM MARSHAL ROMANZOFF'S HEADQUARTERS IN POLAND.

8th June 1788.

"If you inquire, my dear Charles, how I am, I shall reply : Always the same. I am continually with the armies and the marshals, trying to make them do something. But the devil is with them, in spite of all their Russian signs of the cross.

"The best thing I have done is to have left that quiz, that maker of compliments, my admirer, as he calls himself, for Kaminiecz. Ah! if I still had a heart, how terribly in love I should be! The governor's wife,[1] that

---

[1] The famous Sophie de Witt was a Greek slave, stolen from the Island of Chio. She attracted the notice of the French ambassador in a street of Constantinople, and he had her taken care of and educated. On his way to St. Petersburg the ambassador

magnificent Greek, known and admired all over the world, drove me in a berlin within half a cannon's range of Choczim, from whence a few shots were fired over our heads.

" I confess that I felt more inclined to find out her weak point of attack than to reconnoitre that of the fortress.

" I stay at her house ; but what an infernal row goes on ! A rattle of chains all night ; I thought there were ghosts. The fact is that her husband, who is commandant of Kaminiecz, has all his work done by convicts. What a contrast between their rascally countenances and the beauty of her whom

stopped at Kaminiecz ; he had brought Sophie with him. General de Witt, Governor of Bessarabia, entertained the ambassador, and was so struck with the beauty of the Greek slave that he fell desperately in love with her.

In order to deceive his guest, he arranged a hunting party, which was to meet at a great distance from the fortress, and, excusing himself on the ground of a sudden order, remained behind. Hardly had the ambassador left than de Witt closed the gates, and celebrated his marriage with Sophie. On returning in the evening, the ambassador was much surprised to find the gates closed ; an envoy was sent, who informed him of what had taken place ; he thought it useless to contend against an accomplished fact, and philosophically resigned himself to his ward's marriage.

they serve, under the sway of the rod! Even
the cook is a convict; it is economical, but
dreadful.

"I wish, my dear Charles, that Oczakoff
(I must return to Potemkin, for I am still more
incapable of moving this man) may procure
me something glorious in your style. I shall
be killed on your account, for you must have
a father worthy of you. *You thought of me*,
you say; you are sublime and touching. You
have worked for me; I will work for you. I
send you a tender farewell from these five or
six hundred leagues distance."

The Prince found Potemkin and his army
just as he had left them, and he writes to his
son, who had recommended a Prussian officer
to him :—

FROM THE CAMP IN THE DESERTS OF TARTARY.

Before OCZAKOFF, 30*th July*.

"I will place your Prussian officer. I
cannot make Prince Potemkin advance as far
as the Liman, but I can advance officers.

I have made generals, majors, etc. ; but you have made your crop of laurels, and can laugh at me.

"Always the same inaction, one - third through fear, one through spite, and one through ignorance. I would wish, at the end of the war, to have one-quarter of your glory in this campaign. Your letters are gay and brave, like yourself; they bear your image.

"A fearful storm obliges me to go to bed. A cloud has burst over the camp, and inundated the two pretty little houses I have erected under my immense Turkish tent, so that I do not know where to put my foot. Oh, oh! I am this moment informed that a major has been killed by lightning in his tent; it falls nearly every day, catch it who may.

"The other day the arms of an officer of light cavalry had to be amputated on account of the bite of a tarentula ; as for lizards, no one is in a better position than I am to assert that they are the friend of man ; for I live with them, and can trust them better than my friends in this country. Sometimes I hear the wind rising, and have my tent opened, but I shut it up again quickly; for the wind seems to blow off a furnace. Oh! we do enjoy every sort of advantage here. Shall I give you a specimen of Prince Repnin's good taste? You know the habits of the service here, the baseness of the inferiors, and the insolence of the superiors. When Prince Potemkin makes a sign or drops anything, twenty generals prostrate themselves to earth. The other day seven or eight of them tried to help Prince Repnin off with his cloak : ' No, gentlemen,' he said ; 'the Prince de Ligne will kindly do it.' A good lesson! They have more refinement of mind than of heart, and they felt it.

"Nevertheless, I rather play the victim ; but Sarti[1] is here with an excellent orchestra,

---

[1] Sarti (Joseph), a celebrated Italian composer, born at Faënza in 1730. In 1785 he was called to St. Petersburg by Catherine II. Under the protection of Potemkin he was appointed in 1793

and he has brought that music you know so well, in which there are thirty C's, thirty D's, etc.   Sometimes we have no bread, only biscuits and macaroons ; no apples or pears, but pots of jam ; no butter, but ices ; no water, but every kind of wine ; no wood for the kitchen fire sometimes, but logs of aloës to burn for perfume. We have here Madame Michel Potemkin, who is extremely beautiful ; Madame Skawrowski, another niece of the vizier or patriarch Potemkin (for he arranges his religion also), very charming ; and Madame Samoiloff, another niece, still more lovely.   I played a proverb for her in this desert, and she seemed to like it, for she has since said : ' Do play another *riddle* for me.'

" I presented the other day to the Prince a blockhead sent to me by a fool.   One is called Marolles, the other is M. de X——,

Director of the Conservatorium at Catherinoslaff, with an annual revenue of thirty-five thousand roubles ; he was allowed free lodging and fifteen thousand roubles for travelling expenses.   Admitted into the ranks of the Russian nobility, he died at Berlin in 1802.

who recommends him as head of the engineers, and destined to take Oczakoff.

"'Good morning, General,' he said, on entering, to the Prince, 'I will take that place for you in a fortnight. Have you any books here? Do you know in Russia those of a M. Vauban and a certain Coëhorn?[1] I should like to look them over before beginning.' You may fancy Potemkin's astonishment. 'What a man!' he said to me, 'I do not know if he is an engineer, but I know he is French. Ask him a few questions.' I did so, and he admitted he was an engineer for roads and bridges.

" Baron de Stad, who is here, delights me. He also is a thorough Frenchman ; annoying the Prince, unpleasant to every one, writing

---

[1] Coëhorn (Menno, Baron de), celebrated engineer, contemporary and rival of Vauban. He defended Namur against Vauban, and for two days repulsed the attack on Fort Wilhelm, but at last succumbed to superior numbers. He directed, under the Prince de Nassau-Saarbruck's orders, the sieges of Venloo and Ruremonde, which, owing to his skilful operations, were obliged to capitulate. He had a great reputation in Germany. Born in 1641 in Friesland, he died on 17th March 1704.

charming verses, hating the petulance of
Roger,[1] with whom he is perpetually quarrel-
ling, and going gallantly into action, though
declaring all the time that he is dying of
fright. 'Behold,' says he, 'how nature suffers;
my horse himself trembles, and cares no more
for glory than I do.' We have seen another
personage, as ridiculous as his name, which
is Gigandé, a lieutenant in the guards of the
Abbé de Porentruy. Yesterday he was robbed.
Furious, he exclaimed, with his Swiss accent:
'*Che me lèfe, che m'égorge les pieds pour
aller tout te suite faire mes blaintes à un
chéneral et il me tit : 'Si c'est un soltat, che*

---

[1] Comte Roger de Damas (born in 1765, died in 1823). At the
age of fifteen he was already an officer in the French army ; his
bravery, his chivalrous character, his quick intellect, made him the
observed of all. "François First, the great Condé, and the
Marshal de Saxe, would have wished to have a son like him," says
the Prince de Ligne. "In the midst of the heaviest cannonade he
is giddy as a cockchafer, noisy, the most relentless singer, shouting
the finest opera airs, making the maddest quotations in the midst
of the firing, and yet judging perfectly all that goes on. War does
not intoxicate him, but he is full of a genial ardour, such as one
feels after a supper . . . amiable, beloved by all, what is called a
nice Frenchman, good-looking, an excellent fellow, and a well-bred
gentleman of the Court of France : such is Roger de Damas."

vous ferai rentre, mais, si c'est un officier, cela sera tifficile.'[1]

"Another Frenchman, whose name is M. Second, came to consult me about an affair of honour. 'For I see, sir,' he said, 'that I shall be forced to fight!' I assured him that if he spoke in that way to everybody he would have no need of a man of his own name; that was a good piece of nonsense, was it not?

"Shall I tell you one of my innocent amusements? I place my dromedaries in the way of the gilded staff, when by chance *'Marlborough s'en va-t-en guerre'* (Marlborough goes off to the wars).[2] The other day two or three generals were thrown, half the escort upset, and the other half sent flying.

"Ah, Charles, when shall we meet again, at Stamboul or at Bel Œil? If only the Emperor and my Russian General would not

---

[1] "I get up, I become footsore with running about to complain to the general, and he says to me : 'If it is a soldier, your things will be returned ; but if it is an officer, it will be difficult.'"

[2] Popular French song.

stand on such ceremony about crossing the
Save and the Bog as they would do to go
through a door, we should soon upset the
Sublime Porte, and should meet where I said.
Then, my dear Cinéas, etc. etc. In the mean-
while let us love each other wherever we are."

On the Russian side the situation remained the same till October, and during this
time things went as badly as possible for
Austria. This disastrous campaign cost her
thirty thousand men, killed in various engage-
ments, forty thousand carried off by the
plague, the invasion of the Banate, and several defeats in Bosnia. Ill with fatigue, in
despair at his want of success, alarmed at
the complete rebellion in Flanders, Joseph
returned to Vienna almost broken-hearted.
He determined to call to his side the Prince
de Ligne, and to give him, with Marshal
Laudon, the command of his army during the
ensuing campaign. He sent Prince Charles
to carry the order to his father. We can

imagine how welcome was the arrival of the conqueror of Sabacz, and with what transports of delight he was received. His father immediately prepared to depart, and they arrived in Vienna at the end of November. Potemkin took Oczakoff a fortnight later. It seemed as though he had waited Ligne's departure before deciding on the attack, and his jealous character justifies the supposition. The winter was peacefully spent at Vienna, and Prince Charles, absorbed in his new passion, did not seem afflicted at his wife's absence.

In the spring of 1789 the two Princes joined Marshal Laudon's army. General de Ligne commanded the right wing, and played an important part at the siege of Belgrade, during which he displayed an indefatigable energy. "I was all on fire myself," he writes, "urged on by that being,[1] who is more like a god than a man. Urged on by him, I urged on the others. Bolza watched, and

[1] Marshal Laudon.

danced attendance. Funk fired, Maillard[1]
advanced. I thanked, begged, thundered,
threatened, commanded; all was done, and
well done, in the twinkling of an eye."

Prince Charles, who was Colonel, was in
command, and energetically seconded his
father, who caught a violent fever during the
siege, and was confined to his bed for some
days, at which he was very furious. He
writes to Marshal Lascy: " The Turkish
Caïques have been venturing too near Krieg-
Insel (my headquarters). 'We must give
them a lesson,' I said to my son, who at times
engaged with my own, at others with Marshal
Laudon's column of attack; Charles, with
his usual liveliness, immediately threw himself into a boat with my aides-de-camp, and,
followed by about forty other small boats,
went off to attack the Turkish Caïques.

" I directed the battle from my window,
in spite of a diabolical attack of fever, and

---

[1] MM. Bolza, Funk, and Maillard were the Prince's three
aides-de-camp.

almost killed myself screaming to an Italian, who commanded my frigate, the *Marie-Thérèse:* '*Alla larga!*' and words which I dare not write. Out of patience I finally went myself to end this very peculiar naval engagement."

Belgrade was taken on the 8th of October 1789; Prince Charles had again the honour of being first at the assault. Marshal Laudon, who was not lavish of praise or flattery, wrote to the Prince de Ligne the most complimentary letter, in which he said : " More than half the glory won by the taking of Belgrade by right belongs to your Highness."

The Emperor sent the Prince the cross of Commander of the Order of Marie-Thérèse, accompanied by a dry and cold letter, whose purpose de Ligne could not unravel ; but he was still so ill with fever that both cross and letter made but a slight impression. He solved the riddle later on : Joseph II. had unjustly suspected him of having encouraged the rebellion in Flanders.

X

THE Turkish war had seemingly caused a
happy diversion from Polish affairs, and for
the last two or three years that country
had enjoyed a most unusual state of peace.
Russia, entirely absorbed by her important
wars in Turkey and in Sweden, was apparently oblivious of her existence. Austria, on
her side, took little heed, and was satisfied
with the large share that had been ceded
to her in the first dismemberment that had
taken place. But this lull could not continue.
Prussia was secretly making overtures to the
Poles, and trying to prevent Stanislaus from

sending his promised reinforcements to the Russians.

The Polish nobility, always restless and disunited, were anxious to take advantage of Russia's difficulties, but could not agree on the course likely to ensure success. The majority, however, tempted by Prussia's secret promises, were disposed to listen to her advances, and conclude with her a defensive alliance. A new constitution, more in harmony with the actual state of Poland, was also a question of debate, and the public mind, now thoroughly roused, anticipated with increasing interest the meeting of the Diet.[1]

The King summoned it to meet on the 6th of October 1788. The arrival of all the nuncios, accompanied by their numerous retinues, part of which came from the most

---

[1] This Diet was called the Grand or Constitutional Diet; it lasted four years, and decreed hereditary rights to the throne, religious liberty, the maintenance of a permanent army, and a new distribution of taxes, affecting also the nobility. See Ferrand's *History of the Dismemberment of Poland.*

distant Palatinates, imparted to Warsaw an
unusually animated appearance ; and the
town offered at that time attractions of a
most unique character.

The great Polish lords, who habitually
lived on their estates, had retained manners
and customs that partook of an uncivilised
magnificence. They nearly all possessed
palaces in Warsaw, but only inhabited them
during the Diets—that is to say, for six weeks
every two years ; and these large residences
presented the most curious mixture of luxury
and penury. After passing through empty
halls, where the ceilings were falling to pieces,
and the hangings were all mouldy from the
damp, one came upon drawing-rooms with
ornamented frescoes, and with gold and
blue vaulted ceilings. The ante-rooms were
crowded with lacqueys in tattered liveries,
and with poor gentlemen who, attending as
servants upon the great lords, proudly wore
the ancient Polish costumes. Though they
did not give at Warsaw, as in the Pala-

tinates, gigantic feasts, during which the toasts were accompanied by a salute of artillery, yet they did not completely abandon all the old customs, and the master of the house would still occasionally honour the lady of his thoughts by sending round her tiny shoe, full of champagne or Tokay.

The tone of the best French society reigned at the Polish Court with a mixture of oriental peculiarities. European good taste was combined with that of Asia, and the polished manners of civilised countries did not exclude the hospitality common to those beyond the pale.

A revival took place in Polish literature during the reign of Stanislaus-Augustus. The King patronised learning, and encouraged to his utmost the reorganisation of the universities. After the suppression of the Jesuits the funds obtained by the sale of their property were entirely applied to this object. A regular committee was appointed to superintend the national education. The

Bishop of Wilna was one of its most influential members; he created at his own expense a professorship of anatomy at the university of Wilna, which was the first that existed in Poland.[1]

During the reign of Stanislaus-Augustus the Court was celebrated for its pleasures, its love intrigues, and its pretty women; their beauty had become proverbial. Among the beauties of that time were the Princess Lubomirska, whom we have already heard of under the name of Princesse Maréchale; her sister-in-law, the fascinating Princess Czartoryska, a Fleming by birth; the Countess Potocka, an Ossolinska by birth; and the Princess Charles of Courland. The two

[1] The dismemberment of Poland did not arrest the intellectual progress of the nation, which from that time devoted itself to the preservation of the Polish language, and to the protection of the monuments of the country. The influence exercised by Prince Czartoryski in the Emperor Alexander's councils greatly assisted this movement. He purchased the magnificent library of the King Stanislaus-Augustus, which, added to his own, became the most important depository of Slavonic history and literature. It was confiscated by Russia in 1831.

latter were really beautiful, and all four were intelligent women. It was asserted that the first one made the fortune of those she loved, the second robbed them of it, and the two others simply enjoyed themselves without thinking of anything else. The Princess Langorouska and the Countess Branicka, the Princess André Poniatowska, sister-in-law to the King, the Princess Lubomirska, a Haddik by birth, also ranked high at Court, where all the affairs of the State were the mainspring of society. The King, who was weak, indulgent, and always in love, was governed by the favourite of the moment.[1]

---

[1] "It would be necessary," says the Prince de Ligne, "to prevent the ladies at Court from harming the Government by intrigues in love, in politics, and in society ; and also advisable to attract the great lords by all sorts of amusements and distinctions. It would then be possible to retain in the kingdom all the money which the pettiest noble, as soon as he has cut his mustachios and left off his long respectable coat, thinks necessary to carry off to Paris, and spend with women, tailors, hotels, and hairdressers, and in gambling and paying off the police, with whom he is always getting into trouble." Unfortunately the King himself set the example of thus abandoning the ancient Polish customs in favour of the French.

The Prince, during his short stay at Warsaw, soon perceived these weak points, and he says : " The King is too honest a man with women, as he is indeed with all his subjects ; he is genuinely in love, and inconstant with the greatest possible sincerity ; and thus he often throws himself into the arms of his opponents, deserting and ruining his own cause."

Such was the Court at which the Princess Charles was to shine. Her reputation for intelligence, beauty, and coquetry having already attracted the attention of all, her Polish nationality, elegance, talents, and the evident pleasure she showed on returning to her native land, delighted her fellow-countrymen.

Her empty palace, rapidly metamorphosed by her own able hands, became one of the most elegant in Warsaw, and she availed herself of the opportunity to display the remarkable domestic qualities she possessed, and which had been so little appreciated by her mother-in-law. During the latter time of her stay at Bel Œil her husband had forbidden her to ride, on account of her delicate health ; she now amply made up for that privation. The Prince-Bishop, who thoroughly spoilt her, gave her the most beautiful horses, and she might be seen every morning on horseback escorted by several young noblemen who were perfect horsemen, as are all the Poles. She built a theatre in her palace, and gratified her love of acting to her heart's content.

Freed from the supervision that oppressed her at Bel Œil, Hélène abandoned herself without constraint to the irresistible charms of this life of pleasure. She forgot the past, her husband, and her daughter even ; the Princesse Charles de Ligne no longer existed— Hélène Massalska alone remained.

Winter was rapidly drawing to a close, and the Princess still gave no thought to Vienna. The de Ligne family, justly offended at her prolonged absence, preserved a disdainful silence.

The Prince-Bishop had returned to Wilna during the vacation of the Diet, but his niece, who wished to enjoy the summer season, just then beginning, remained alone at Warsaw.

The King, his family, and the most important personages at Court, had elegant country-houses in the suburbs, where they indulged in the most sumptuous and original festivities. The greatest luxury was displayed in these entertainments, where each host endeavoured to surpass his neighbour in planning surprises and unforeseen effects. The first one at which the Princess Charles appeared was given by the Princess André Poniatowska. "The heat on that day had been suffocating; the Prince led his visitors to a grotto formed by an artificial rock, from which fell a cascade, imparting by its very sound a cool and agreeable sensation. Then they all went into the grotto, where they rested for a few minutes on the soft mossy banks, after which the Prince proposed a walk in the park. They entered

a shady avenue leading to a door, which was
hidden in the foliage; he touched a spring,
the door flew open, and disclosed a magnificent circular hall, splendidly illuminated, and
painted with frescoes representing allegorical
subjects; it was surrounded by niches in the
walls containing Turkish divans, which were
covered with the richest brocades. The back
of these recesses was of a dead gold, contrast-
ing marvellously with the black hair and delicate complexion of the Polish ladies who came
to rest in them. They had barely seated
themselves when strains of music were heard,
which seemed to descend mysteriously from
the skies. Suddenly the floor opened, and a
table, magnificently laid out, slowly ascended,
as if at the touch of a fairy's wand." The
King seated himself, and motioned the desired guests to their places, Princesse Hélène
being among the number.

Stanislaus was most agreeably disposed;
he was fond of conversation, and set every
one at ease. He liked to speak on art and

literature ; his mind, which was cultivated, though without much depth, appeared at these entertainments under its most favourable aspect.   Paris and France were the topics of conversation, and as they recalled the delightful past, the King took pleasure in questioning Hélène about the people whom he had known.

When supper was over they again went into the park, and wandered about in the beautiful moonlight, returning only to Warsaw when the night was far advanced.

Hélène had become particularly intimate with the Princess Czartoryska, so passionately loved by Lauzun, and of whom he has left a charming description.[1]   The Princess's residence was entirely different from any of the others ; for Powinski was laid out in what we now call the *realistic* style.

Each member of the family occupied a cottage, the exact reproduction of a peasant's

---

[1] See the *Memoirs* of Lauzun, whose authenticity, however, one can by no means be certain of.

hut; it was made with trunks of trees laid
one on the other, cemented together by
a mixture of earth and straw: "Madame
la Princesse inhabited a very large hut;
those of the children and servants were
smaller. This group of cottages looked like
a village in the midst of an immense park;
but, on entering one of them, one was struck
by the sumptuousness of the apartments
which greeted the eye. The finish and
elegance of the decorations were on a
scale of which one single detail will give
an idea. The bathroom of the Princess
was lined from top to bottom with tiles
of Dresden china, painted with the utmost delicacy, and each representing a small
picture: they numbered, it is said, three
thousand.

"After leaving these would-be cottages, and
crossing a part of the park, one came upon an
enormous Turkish tent, of a magnificent and
curious appearance. It had belonged to the
Vizier, and was taken during the war be-

tween the Russians and the Turks. The interior was ornamented with Oriental hangings and trophies of Turkish arms, which were exceedingly beautiful. On the ground were rich carpets, and piles of gold-embroidered cushions used as seats made the illusion perfect. Behind the heavy curtains sounds of Turkish music were heard, and servants dressed in Eastern costumes served pipes and coffee on small low tables, inlaid with mother-of-pearl." Every reception-day the park, lakes, rivers, and bridges were illuminated, and supper was served the whole evening in a large pavilion covered with creepers, and open on all aides. A number of small tables were laid out, and at each one of the ladies presided. A ball was organised in the Princess's cottage, where they danced most of the night.

After enjoying these gaieties for some time, Hélène joined her uncle at Werky. With the exception of a few short holidays, the Diet, contrary to the usual custom, sat without interruption and without fresh elections till the year 1792. During these four years, and notwithstanding the critical nature of the political questions under discussion, the Court of Stanislaus presented an unusually brilliant aspect, which, however, was not destined to last.

While the Diet was sitting all the Crown officials were obliged by their duties to reside in Warsaw. Amongst those who attracted the most notice was the Lord High Chamberlain, Count Vincent Potocki. He belonged to one of the most illustrious families in Poland, and possessed immense landed estates and palaces of regal magnificence. His father, Stanislaus-Potocki, Palatine of Kiew, was the nephew and godson of the King Stanislaus-Leczinski, and therefore first cousin of the late Queen of France.

Although at this time the Lord Chamberlain was nearly thirty-eight years of age, he passed for one of the most fascinating men at Court. Gifted with a keen and refined intellect, very careful of his own interests, a favourite with women, and always on the best of terms with influential men, he knew the art of being successful with every one.

His first wife was Ursule Zamoiska,[1] niece of King Stanislaus-Augustus; they had no children, and were divorced at the end of a few years. Divorces were of such frequent occurrence in Poland, and had become such an established custom, that this event made no difference in the Count's position with the King. Shortly after her divorce Princess Zamoiska married the Count Mniseck, and Count Vincent himself married in 1786 the Countess Micielska, by whom he had two sons. It was just at the time of the birth of his second son that the Count was summoned by his duties to War-

[1] The King's eldest sister, Louise Poniatowska, married Count J. J. Michel Zamoiski, by whom she had one daughter, Ursule Zamoiska. Madame Geoffrin wrote as follows to King Stanislaus on 25th March 1776 :—" Society at Warsaw is more brilliant than ever—at least I hear of a great many marriages. Your niece, Mademoiselle Ursule Zamoiska, is marrying a Count Potocki, brother-in-law of a Countess Potocka who is here."

saw.   The Countess remained at Ukrania, in a property near Niemirow, their habitual residence, her health not yet permitting her to travel.

The Lord Chamberlain, on arriving at Warsaw, met the Princesse Hélène at his cousins, Mesdames Jean and Severin Potocka; he was presented to her, and soon became one of the most faithful followers of her little Court.   Hitherto Hélène, like a real coquette, had noticed all her admirers without seeming to distinguish any, but it was soon apparent that she received Count Vincent with marked favour.   Her habits changed entirely, she went much less into society, and was only seen at the houses which the Count himself habitually frequented. He showed the greatest reserve in his intercourse with the Princess.   Either from policy or prudence, he manifested no eagerness, and even affected to avoid meeting her too often; it was easy, however, for an attentive observer to see that he was flattered at the distinction with which he was treated by a young, beautiful, and most attractive woman.

Hélène, who was in love for the first time in her life, gave herself up completely to the feelings which influenced her. Without admitting it to herself, she felt keenly the Count's coldness of manner towards her, and endeavoured to find out its cause; she thought he disapproved of her worldly pursuits, and she hoped to please him by giving them up : the pleasure parties, the brilliant cavalcades, were all abandoned. She courted solitude, and in her letters to her friends betrayed, unawares, her secret thoughts : here is an answer from the Princesse Henri Lubomïrska, then living in Paris, which shows that her passion was no longer a secret :—

PARIS, 15*th October* 1789.

"At last, pussie, I have received a letter from you, dated the 24th of September. It is a thousand and a hundred thousand years

since I had heard from you, and I even felt
a little cross, I must confess. But, after
seeing in your letter such big phrases as
actual situation, settled for ever, etc., I have
cooled down, for, like Germain in *La Feinte
par Amour*,[1] 'What I am not told I know
nevertheless.' Really I am sorry that I
cannot see you in *this new situation, which
makes solitude* so precious. You must be
very funny, not that I think the sentimental
style altogether unbecoming to you; there
are privileged beings whom every phase
suits, and this can be said of you more than
of anybody; but I cannot suppress a certain
curiosity,—forgive me for it, my pet. Your
happiness is my most ardent wish, and I am
more interested than ever in desiring it, since
the longer it lasts the longer you will remain
with us. Tell me what terms you are on
with Madame de Mniseck ;[2] I have good

[1] *La Feinte par Amour*, The Counterfeit of Love, comedy in
three acts and verse by Dorat, played for the first time on 13th
July 1773.

[2] Ursule Zamoiska, Count Potocki's first wife.

reasons for asking, and you will understand them ; but do not mention my question to anybody, and when you see the Lord Chamberlain, present him with my compliments.

" Is it true that he is irrevocably settled at Warsaw, and has given up Niemirow ?

" By the bye, why were you astonished that in a letter dated from Paris I should have sent you the Comte Auguste's[1] compliments? It was not on the high-road, but here, where he is deputy at the States-General, that I saw him. I will not mention my health ; it is too tiresome a subject. Neither will I write about what goes on here, as political matters do not interest you much ; and, moreover, you see everything in the newspapers. So good-bye, my puss ; write often ; you know that your letters are always a great pleasure to me. Are you still fond of riding and

---

[1] Comte Auguste de la Marck, second son of the Duchesse d'Aremberg. A friend of Mirabeau, he played an interesting part in the commencement of the Revolution.

going to the theatre ?　I am afraid you have
given up all these amusements.　Forgive my
surmises; at a distance of five hundred
leagues one may sometimes make a mistake,
and see things in a wrong light; but at least
believe that no distance can diminish the
tender interest I feel for you."

Evidently Hélène's friend knew perfectly
all that was going on; her question with
regard to the Comtesse de Mniseck proves it.
She wished to know on what footing the two
young women were with each other.　Hélène
had naturally become intimate with her.
Madame de Mniseck was only too glad that
the Count should be faithless to her successor.
We have already seen that Hélène was
extremely worried by the Count's coldness
and reserve towards herself; she could not
refrain from mentioning it to Madame de
Mniseck, who, according to the singular
Polish habit, had remained on perfectly
courteous terms with her first husband.　It

is not necessary to add that the word *love* was never mentioned between them ; they only recognised an "affectionate regard," and Hélène implored her friend to discover the cause of the Count's strange behaviour. Madame de Mniseck graciously fulfilled this strange commission, and reassured Hélène so completely that she wrote as follows to the Count :—

"Madame de Mniseck has just told me that you have spoken of me in affectionate terms to her, and that you reproach yourself with having left me for three months in doubt as to your sentiments.

"I am deeply touched at this ; your affection is precious to me, and will always be so, and, as I felt that I had not been in fault, I was sure your good heart would bring you back to me sooner or later."

It is evident that little by little the intimacy between the Count and Hélène was increasing. Perhaps he was unconsciously fascinated by the very great charm

of the young Princess ?   Perhaps in the
Bishop of Wilna's immense fortune he hoped
to find a resource for freeing his lands from
their heavy mortgages ?   It is difficult to tell,
for, in this circumstance, as in all those connected with the Count, the motive of his
conduct remains an enigma.

Whatever the reason, he accepted the
delicate responsibility of managing Hélène's
affairs, which had been in a state of great
confusion for some time.   The Count had
an undoubted capacity for business—a rare
quality in a Polish noble ; they generally
know how to spend their fortune better
than how to manage it.

The advice which he gave the Princess
was a pretext for frequent interviews, which
always took place in the presence of a third
person, either a secretary or a young lady.[1]
One day, however, Hélène received a note

[1] The great Polish ladies were always accompanied by some
young girl or young married woman, who belonged to the lesser
and poorer nobility ; their position was that of a companion or
even head lady's-maid.

from the Count begging for a private interview. Surprised and disturbed at the receipt
of these few lines, Hélène, without reflecting
on their undoubted significance, replied that
she would grant his request, but only on
condition that he would remember she was
another man's wife.

The Count arrived at the appointed time,
and after a few minutes of the most trivial
conversation, Hélène, agitated and trembling,
asked him, without reflecting on the purport
of her words, why he had demanded this
interview. He answered rather coldly that
she appeared to be aware of it already ; and
he then made her a regular declaration. The
young Princess, carried away by the violence
of her feelings, admitted that she loved him
as she had never loved any one before, but
that she was determined that this confession
should lead to no result so long as they had
not each recovered their liberty.

The Count calmly replied that he was
proud of the distinction conferred, that it was

sufficient for his happiness, and that his reserve and respect would prove that he was an honourable man. He then made a deep obeisance and retired, leaving Hélène in a most agitated frame of mind.

She felt more humiliated than satisfied with what had taken place ; for, in accordance with a very natural sentiment, she had wished to maintain a discreet behaviour, with the intention of taking all the credit to herself ; she had prepared to combat an ardent lover, and she had found herself face to face with a man who was able not only to master his feelings, but was even more reasonable than she was.

Dissatisfied with herself, with him, and with the rash admission she had just made, she wrote and tore up three or four letters after his departure ; at last she sent him the following :—

" I have tried three times to write to you, without having been able to express the agitation of my heart. How changed are my prospects since yesterday! I feel humiliated, degraded. . . . I granted the very first request you made, but I wished to place between us a barrier which your delicacy of feeling would respect. On reflection I perceive that my surrender has only added to my imprudence. I have shown you my weakness, whilst you have shown me how honour should control nature. I forgot myself whilst you remembered; this is not the moment to claim your esteem, time alone will restore it to me.

"*P.S.*—My thoughts are so full of yesterday's events that I have not been able to close my eyes. Can it be possible that a single day should thus influence my life; I feel that, henceforth, it is yours, and yours alone!"

Hélène spoke truly, for this affection, already so deeply rooted, was to last all her life.

It appears that the Count replied in a way that sufficed to dispel the anxiety of the young Princess ; for he received the following note from her, which we find carefully preserved amongst her other letters.[1]

" The few words you have written have filled me with joy. I read and reread them ten times whilst dressing, and I found the pastime a sweet one. I shall see you this evening at Madame Jean's."[2]

We do not possess any of the letters which the Count wrote at that time ; but, judging by Hélène's answers, he must have been a jealous and despotic man. She submitted to his tyranny in a most extraordinary manner. He insisted on her burning all the letters she had received from her husband and her friends, and made so severe a selection among her numerous acquaintances at Warsaw, that little by little he narrowed her sphere to a small circle, in which he reigned supreme ; Hélène accepted everything.

---

[1] Hélène's notes, many of which were insignificant, were docketed and carefully kept by the Count.

[2] Madame Jean Potocka, the Count's niece.

"I wrote to you last night, and intended sending off my note this morning," she writes, "but when I awoke it was too late.

"What is it that worries you? Tell me at once. If a complete sacrifice of all that displeases you can secure your peace of mind, say but one word, and it will cost me nothing. I shall consider myself the gainer if, by giving up everything, I am able to make you happy and contented.

"If these ladies had not insisted on my going with them, I would willingly have stayed at home.

"With you alone I have enough to occupy my heart and mind without requiring the presence of others."

About this time, that is, towards the end of 1790, the Comtesse Vincent, who had completely recovered her health, left Ukrania, and joined her husband at Warsaw. It was impossible to prevent her return, and equally impossible to conceal from her the growing intimacy between the Lord Chamberlain and the Princesse de Ligne, whose reputation of coquetry and beauty had already reached her ears.

The Comtesse Anna adored her husband, and in spite of all his efforts to hide the truth from her she soon discovered it, and absolutely refused to admit the Princess within her doors. "I shall never consent," she said to her husband, "to receive the woman who has robbed me of your affection, whatever may be the nature of your intimacy." The Count, very much surprised at this unexpected resistance on her part, vainly endeavoured to dispel his wife's suspicion, but when Hélène called on the Countess she found the door closed. Mortally wounded by this affront, she gave way to all the violence of her character; she declared to the Count that she insisted on his compelling his wife to receive her, adding that she could never rest under an insult that dishonoured her in the eyes of the world. The Count, after trying in vain to calm her, finally flew into a

passion, and after a terrible scene abruptly
left her. Utterly upset by the manner in
which the Count had left her on the previous day, Hélène sent him the very next
morning these few lines, written in such a
state of agitation as to be almost illegible :—

"I am writing to you without knowing how
to begin. What a scene! I am still quite
unnerved by it ; you have left me, abandoned
me, and nothing remains to alleviate my
despair. I am alone in the world. I have
neglected my friends, broken all ties, burnt
under your eyes all the proofs of the affection
which my husband once bestowed on me. I
have destroyed secrets, confidences, assurances
of tenderness from the friends of my childhood,
and yesterday you retracted the few words of
affection which have at times escaped your
lips. Who will console me in my affliction ?
I leave it to you to imagine what remains
after this. Good-bye, my dear Vincent ; in
any case, should I meet you again, you will
always be the eternal object of my affections,

and should nothing bring you back to me, that of my eternal regrets. In any case you alone will occupy all my thoughts, and possess till death all my affection.

"If you are determined never to see me again, return my letters, and at the end of this one write: *Adieu.* This sentence, to be decreed by your hand, is the only favour I solicit from you."

This note was returned to the Princess, a few minutes later, by the messenger who had taken it. The seal was unbroken,[1] but on it were traced two lines, in the Comtesse Anna's own handwriting, with the following words: "The Count left this morning for Niemirow." This news filled Hélène with dismay; she fancied the Countess rejoicing at her grief, triumphing in his departure, and preparing to join her husband and her children. A mad idea shot through her brain; she rang at once, and

---

[1] We have found this letter amongst the Count's papers. Hélène probably forwarded it before she determined to join him.

ordered a post-chaise to be brought round immediately. Half an hour later the Princess threw herself into the carriage, accompanied by only one of her women, and after a journey of astounding rapidity arrived at Niemirow a few hours after the Count.

The latter had left Warsaw merely to escape from a position that was no longer bearable, and without any settled resolution. The unexpected arrival of Hélène completely unnerved him ; her beauty, her tenderness, her despair, the rashness of her conduct in thus sacrificing her reputation, all combined to move and perplex him, and the recollection of poor Comtesse Anna could not contend against the fascination of the moment. Hélène carried the day, and when the emotion of the first few moments was over they agreed to ask for a divorce on both sides.

The Princess, dreading lest the Count should change his mind, urged that their plans should be carried out without delay, and the very next day three letters were despatched from Niemirow, the first addressed to the Comtesse Anna, the second to the Prince de Ligne, and the third to the Bishop of Wilna. The Count offered his wife the custody of their two sons, besides a large annuity, if she would consent to the divorce. The Princess requested that her daughter Sidonie should be sent back to her, and that the Prince-Bishop and a trustee appointed by her, and invested with her full authority, should settle all questions of interest with the de Ligne family. Then, in a letter to her uncle, she informed him of her intended divorce, asking him not to withdraw his sympathy from her, and help her in the settlement of her affairs.

The Comtesse Anna was in total ignorance of what had taken place; her husband's letter told her the sad truth. The unhappy woman could as yet hardly believe in the reality of the blow which had fallen upon her. She had scarcely been married four years, and her unvarying gentleness and blameless char-

acter ought to have secured to her the last-
ing affection of the husband she adored, and
whose fondest wish had been fulfilled by the
birth of two sons.   She still hoped that this
intimacy would be but a passing fancy, and
refused to consent to a divorce.

Her answer was simple and touching :—

" Have you forgotten," she said, "that we
married out of mutual sympathy, and not
only with the consent but by the wish of our
parents ?   These ties were to last for ever ;
and God sanctioned and blessed them by
granting us children.   You have sometimes
been weak, but I shall still persevere, being
fully persuaded that both my duty and my
happiness are involved. . . .

"I shall always remember that when Francis was born you were on your knees in the
adjoining room, praying to God for me and
for our child.   You loved us then, and if you
searched your inmost heart, you would still
find these two sentiments there, for I believe
nothing could ever efface them.

"You see my heart and soul laid bare before you; read your own; one word, only one, and I will forget everything; I await it with the greatest impatience.

"Your very humble and very obedient servant,   ANNA POTOCKA."

This letter and many others remained without effect; the Lord Chamberlain had already made up his mind. Not only was he completely under the charm of Hélène's fascination, but, as we said before, the prospect of the immense fortune she would possess singularly strengthened his determination.

XI

The rebellion in Flanders—Death of Joseph II.—Prince Charles
in the Russian service—The storming of Ismaïl—Return to
Vienna—Hélène at Kowalowska—The Count's journey to
Paris—The Lignes refuse to grant a divorce—The Count's
illness.

WHILE these romantic events were taking
place in Ukrania others of a more serious
nature were occurring in Flanders. Van der
Noot, uniting his efforts to those of Vonck
and Van der Mersch, had issued a manifesto exhorting the people of Brabant to
rebellion, and on the same day, the 24th of
October 1789, the little army of patriots
assembled at Hasselt had invaded the Belgian territory.[1] The Emperor, suddenly

---

[1] Van der Noot, an active and zealous lawyer, but with more
ambition than capacity, together with the *Grand Pénitencier*, Van
Eupen, headed the party who wished for the maintenance of the

alarmed, tried to arrest the movement by making useless concessions ; the violent irritation he felt at the defection of Flanders caused him to suspect every one belonging to the country of taking part in the rebellion. The Prince de Ligne himself, then at the siege of Belgrade, did not escape his displeasure, and it was then that he wrote him the harsh letter we have already mentioned. But Joseph soon recognised the injustice of his suspicions, and the Prince de Ligne was recalled. The latter obeyed at once, and wrote the following charming letter to the Emperor :—

BELGRADE, *November* 1789.

" I am overjoyed at your Majesty's kindness in permitting me to appear before you, and to remain in Vienna until I start for Moravia or Silesia at the head of the army now returning from Syrmia. I am far more

ancient, aristocratic, and sacerdotal constitution, while another lawyer, Vonck, a man of great ability, and General Van der Mersch, led the popular faction.

touched, Sire, by a grace than by a dis-
grace.   The cares of the siege of Belgrade,
and the fever from which I suffered, that no
amount of quinine could subdue, prevented
my feeling the grief I should naturally have
had on reading the terrible phrase : ' Prepare
yourself to receive marks of my displeasure,
for it is neither my pleasure nor my habit to
be disobeyed.'   I had reason to congratulate
myself on my behaviour, Sire, during the Bavarian war eleven years ago, and you thanked
me for it.   On this occasion, it is true, your
Majesty decided that my despatches should be
conveyed to you through an orderly ; but if I
made use of my aides-de-camp, it was solely
on account of the Comte de Choiseul's special
message from Constantinople, recommending
that his very important despatch to the Marquis de Noailles should be conveyed as safely
and directly as possible.   An orderly may fall
asleep, get drunk, or be murdered.

"I must crave your pardon, Sire, if I
showed no anxiety at your displeasure, but I

know your justice still better ; I supposed that the ill-timed journey made by one of my aides-de-camp to Flanders when the rebellion was at its height had perhaps led your Majesty to suppose that I was concerned in it, and that I had some understanding with the disaffected."[1]

Whilst the Prince de Ligne was returning to Vienna the insurgents seized Ghent and Brussels, and on the 2d of December 1789 they proclaimed that Joseph II. had forfeited the sovereignty of the Netherlands. Two months later the Emperor succumbed to a chronic disease, aggravated by grief and

---

[1] The Belgians had, nevertheless, made the most brilliant offers to the Prince. Van der Noot implored him to come and place himself at their head. "I thank you for the provinces you offer me," he replied in his usual jesting manner, "but I never revolt in winter." Moreover the Prince, who did not approve of revolutions, was indignant at that of Flanders. "If I were there," he writes, "I should speak first as a patriot, a word that is becoming odious to me, then as a citizen, another word often misapplied ; and if I did not succeed I should speak as an Austrian general, and forthwith silence an archbishop, a bishop, a fat monk, a professor, a brewer, and a lawyer."

anxiety.[1] The Prince de Ligne wrote to the
Empress Catherine: "He is no more, Madame,
—he is no more, the Prince who honoured the
man, the man who still more honoured the
Prince. He said to me a few days before
his death, on my return from the Hungarian
army which I had led into Silesia: 'I was
not fit to see you yesterday; your country has
killed me. . . . The capture of Ghent is
my agony, and the abandonment of Brussels
my death. What an outrage' (he repeated
that word several times). 'I am dying of it :
one would have to be of stone to survive it.
I thank you for all you have done for me.
Laudon has spoken very well of you ; I thank
you for your fidelity. Go into Flanders ;

---

[1] The Empress Catherine wrote to Grimm : "Joseph II. killed
himself with his endless audiences ; they are, to say the least, useless,
and waste a great deal of time. I used to tell him so. He was
acquainted with everything, except the disposition of the Flemish
people when the rebellion broke out. I witnessed his astonishment
when the first news arrived ; he came to consult me, and was disposed to treat the affair as a trifling matter ; but I took the liberty
of advising him to pay it the most serious attention." Joseph II.
died on 20th February 1790.

bring back the country to its allegiance. If
you cannot succeed, remain there; do not
sacrifice your interests to me—you have
children. . . .' "

On the Emperor's table were found
several letters, written on the eve of his
death. One of them, which was in French,
was addressed to the Princesses François
and Charles de Lichtenstein, and to the
Comtesses Clary, de Kinsky, and de Kaunitz.

To the Five Ladies who so kindly
received Me into their Society.

" The time has come for me to bid you an
eternal farewell, and express all the gratitude
I feel at the condescension and kindliness
you have shown me for so many years. The
memory of each day is dear to me, and the
thought of separation is the only one that
troubles me. Wholly trusting in the goodness of Providence, I submit myself entirely
to its decrees. Keep me in remembrance,
and do not forget me in your prayers. My

writing will show you the condition I am in."

The Prince de Ligne was deeply affected by this loss, of which he soon felt the painful results.   Leopold II., who succeeded his father, behaved with marked coldness towards all those for whom Joseph had had any affection.   Moreover, the new sovereign's policy had nothing in common with that of his predecessor.   On the 27th of July 1790 Austria signed at Reichenbach a Convention with Prussia, by which she agreed to make peace with Turkey, the conditions to be based on the *status quo* that existed before the war.

Prince Charles, foreseeing a period of forced inaction, asked and obtained permission to enter the Russian service.   He accordingly set off, leaving his father in Vienna unfavourably looked upon at Court, and grieved at being separated from him.

It was under Souvarof's orders in Bess-

arabia that Prince Charles fought his campaign.   He was selected to conduct part of
the operations at the famous siege of Ismaïl.[1]

Since the 19th Souvarof had been batter-
ing the walls of the town; he directed in
person the assault by land, while another
attack was being made from the river.
Three times the Russians were driven back
under a terrific fire; two columns remained
for three hours in the trenches exposed to a
perfect storm of grape shot.   At last a fire
broke out in the town, and the Russians
were able to enter, the assault having lasted
ten hours.   Prince Charles was amongst the
first to go up, and behind him followed, as
simple volunteers, the Duc de Richelieu,
the Comte Roger de Damas, the Comte
de Langeron, etc. etc.   Fifteen thousand

---

[1] Ismaïloff, a town of Russia in Europe (Bessarabia), situated on
the Danube.   The storming of Ismaïl is one of the most celebrated
in history.   The Russians, numbering 30,000, took possession of
the town on 22d November 1790, and pillaged it for three days.
The Russians, exasperated at the resistance they had met with,
massacred two-thirds of the inhabitants.

Turks were massacred, and the town was given up to pillage.   Prince Charles received a wound in the leg, which, however, did not stop him.

General Ribas, who commanded the flotilla in the Danube, wrote to the Prince de Ligne as follows :—

ISMAÏL, 15*th December.*

" MY PRINCE—In recalling myself to the notice of your serene Highness, I venture to congratulate you on the glory that Prince Charles has won at the storming of Ismaïl. The column he commanded, following the example of its daring leader, was the first to effect a landing.   In spite of a severe wound in his leg he was the first to leap out of the boat, and he scaled the ramparts of the town under a deadly fire.   He took possession of it, after setting fire to a Turkish frigate that was doing us great damage, and after establishing and directing the battery, which inflicted the greatest loss on the enemy."

At the moment of Prince Charles's entry into Ismaïl, and in the midst of the fire and pillage and the fearful carnage, he saw a child three or four years old standing alone under the doorway of a fine-looking house, and uttering the most heartrending cries; his beauty and the richness of his attire attracted the attention of the Prince; he took up the child in his arms; it ceased crying, and looked at him with eyes full of astonishment; then, terrified at the tumult and the horrible scenes going on around them, he hid his face on his deliverer's breast, clinging to his neck with all the strength of his little arms. Much moved, the Prince hastily carried the child to a place of safety, and had it questioned by some prisoners who had escaped the massacre. All he could say was that he was called Norokos, and that his mother and the women who took care of him had been killed. The Prince chose among the prisoners a Turkish man and woman, gave the child into their keeping, and commanded that he should receive every possible care, as he had decided to adopt him, and take him to Vienna on his return.

Immediately after the taking of Ismaïl the Empress Catherine wrote to Prince Charles to tell him herself of his promotion to the rank of colonel, and to confer on him the cross of commander of the order of Saint Georges.

The Prince de Ligne was at Vienna when he received the news of the capture of Ismaïl, and of the honours the Empress had bestowed on his son. He had just been slighted and treated with flagrant injustice by Leopold II., but he forgot everything on hearing of his Charles's success, and wrote the same day to the Czarina :—

" MADAME—My heart, which bounds forward so quickly that my pen is unable to keep pace with it, can never sufficiently express my gratitude for the favours bestowed by your Imperial Majesty on my excellent and fortunate Charles. I shall not publish the letter you have deigned to write to me, but shall content myself with never forgetting it. Not until we have peace will your Majesty regain your former wit, as during the last four years you have been all soul and genius. Good heavens, what abundant proof of it there is in your letter to my good Charles! I am afraid it will have put him quite beside himself. . . ."

But it is with his son that the Prince gives himself up to the full vehemence of his feelings.

VIENNA, 25*th November* 1790.

"So you end the war, as you began it, by making me die of anxiety on behalf of the most courageous of mortals, of joy at possessing such a son, of emotion at your conduct, and of regret at never having equalled your merit in any quarter.[1] My dear Charles, in spite of these four deaths, I am quite alive,

---

[1] Prince Charles was extremely modest. His father wrote to Madame de Coigny : " I do not underrate my courage, which may

and the happiest of men, for I am going to
see you again.   My God! good Charles,
brave Charles, what anxiety you have given
me!   Mine is the high stake!   If they
had *néboïsséd* [1] you, as they sometimes do
(and for two or three nights especially the
thought deprived me of sleep), say, what
in the world would have become of me?
Supposing I had survived, could I have
existed a minute without reproaching myself
for my strength and weakness in not opposing
your departure? . . ."

Almost immediately after the peace of Ismaïl
the Empress began secretly to negotiate a
treaty with the Turks.   Preoccupied by events
in France, and especially in Poland, she was
anxious to be rid of a war which absorbed the

---

be brilliant enough, but it is not unalloyed; there is a certain
amount of humbug about it; I perform too much for the public.
How infinitely I prefer the courage of my dear, good Charles, who
never looks to see if he is being looked at."

[1] A Turkish expression, indicating the act of beheading the dead
on the field of battle.

greatest part of her army. Prince Charles, aware of what was going on, asked and obtained his discharge. He announced his return to Vienna to his father, and came back escorted by a numerous retinue. He brought with him the little Norokos and his attendants, a Turkish band of twelve musicians, and magnificent presents of arms and horses that Marshal Souvarof and Prince Potemkin had given him.

The Prince de Ligne to his Son.

" Good Lord! dear Charles! you are coming back, but I cannot realise it. I assure you that since you have had the good fortune to escape from such dangers, you must be physically immortal as well as morally. I do not know how I shall manage to kiss you, how I shall place myself, where your large nose will go, how I shall manage my own ; I fully intend also kissing your wounded knee, perhaps going down on my own knees for the purpose, before you as well as before heaven."

P.S.—To the bravest and prettiest fellow among the Volunteers.[1]

"As for you, my dear Duke, I shall not seek to express the feelings I entertain on your behalf. It is impossible to be a more worthy grandson of the Maréchal de Richelieu, never has any one had a more valiant and charming comrade. Both you and Charles have equally contributed to each other's glory.

---

[1] The Comte de Chinon, Armand-Emmanuel-Sophie-Septimanie Duplessis, Duc de Richelieu, grandson of the Marshal, born the 25th September 1766, died the 16th May 1822. At the age of fourteen he married Mademoiselle de Rochechouart, but had no children by her. The Duke emigrated in 1790, went to Vienna, where he was received with distinction, and from thence to Saint Petersburg, where he was equally well received. "He possessed," says the Prince de Ligne, "rare beauty, and a character of extreme gentleness. Though he did not inherit his grandfather's superior talents, he had nevertheless a sound judgment, many natural virtues, and an ardent love of justice; he was less dissipated than his youthful companions, although fond of ladies' society, and born to please." The Duc de Richelieu was President of the Privy Council under the Restoration.

" Certain of your mutual esteem, you strove
to augment it.　What happiness for me, dear
Duke, to know that you are full of life and
energy ; to remember that I have loved you
from the time of your birth, for hardly had
you come into the world than you were
already its ornament.

" But I must tell you both about the King
of Naples.　What a kind good man he is !
He embraced me about ten times, that is to
say, as often as he met me during the ball,
which took place at the house of his ambassador Gallo.[1]　He took me up to every
one, saying : ' *Suo figlio ! ah ! bravo juvene !
è férito.*' " [2]

The Flemish rebellion was drawing to a
close.　After shaking off the Austrian yoke
the first act of the Flemish people had
been to divide into two hostile factions,

---

[1] The Marquis del Gallo, Neapolitan ambassador at Vienna,
gave this ball in honour of the betrothal of the King of Naples's
two daughters with two Archdukes, sons of the Emperor Leopold.

[2] " His son, ah ! brave young fellow ! is wounded."

one of which was anxious to preserve the ancient, aristocratic, and sacerdotal constitution, to retain which had been the motive of the revolution, while the other faction supported the new doctrines of the constituent assembly in Paris. Leopold, who had learnt the art of negotiating in Tuscany, and was an astute politician, cleverly took advantage of the division of opinions, and on coming to the throne[1] promised to restore to Flanders all her ancient privileges, but at the same time despatched an army strong enough to subdue her if necessary. The country offered no resistance.[2]

On the 2d of December 1790 Leopold granted a general amnesty, and before many months had passed all trace of the disturbances in Flanders had disappeared.

---

[1] The 30th September 1790.

[2] The Comte de Browne took back Brussels from the Belgian patriots with a few companies of grenadiers and a handful of hussars. By dint of care, firmness, and gold, which he distributed in handfuls, he so completely re-established order and security in the town that it became more quiet, more submissive, and more prosperous than it ever had been. (*Unpublished Memoirs of the Prince de Ligne.*)

After enjoying for some time the happiness of seeing her son, the Princesse de Ligne left for Brussels and Bel Œil, in order to repair the damages these residences had sustained during the revolution, for they had been abandoned ever since 1787. It was precisely at this period that Hélène's letters asking for a divorce reached her husband.

The de Ligne family had several times expressed their displeasure at the prolonged stay of the Princesse Charles in Poland. At first she had answered evasively, then, having inquired after her little daughter Sidonie, she ceased writing altogether.

Hélène's sudden departure and prolonged stay in Ukrania had created a great sensation in Warsaw. The Princesse Maréchale and other great ladies, who were spending the winter in Vienna, related the adventure, and commented upon it. The Lignes, as may easily be supposed, were greatly offended at Hélène's imprudent escapade, and, far from favourably receiving her request for a divorce, they absolutely refused to consent to it. It may be supposed that if the lady whom he loved had been free, Prince Charles would have sent a different answer, but there existed, evidently, some insurmountable obstacle to their union. Meanwhile the Count, who directed all Hélène's affairs, started for Paris, invested by her with full powers to treat with the Lignes; for the Princesse Charles was still under the delusion that her request would be granted. On his arrival in Paris he had a first interview with the Prince de Ligne's steward, and gave him a copy of his deed of authorization.

The steward went off at once to confer with the Prince on these grave questions, but when he returned to Paris he found that the Count, who in the meantime had heard from Hélène of Prince Charles's decided refusal, had already taken his departure.

The following is the letter the steward had brought.

Letter from the Prince de Ligne.

Vienna, 15th January 1791.

"As we no longer are aware of the Princesse Charles de Ligne's existence, and as, in fact, she is dead to us and to our little Sidonie, we can enter into no arrangements with her.

"A woman kept prisoner by a stupid Polish tyrant should not prevent Sidonie's great-uncle from paying the bills of exchange, for which he has given us every possible security, and which, according to the desire of Prince Charles and the Prince - Bishop, and even according to that of her mother, are destined to free the estates in Galicia. She has neither the power nor the right to administer these estates, as she is under the influence of a man who publicly manages her business, for in so doing she might damage her daughter's interests.

"When she chooses to free herself from the bondage in which she is living, and take up her residence either in Paris or Warsaw, or on one of my estates if she prefers it, she shall receive an annuity of thirty thousand French livres, which is the least her husband intends her to have, as soon as he shall himself come into the whole of his fortune.

"As the Princesse Charles, if she married the Count Potocki, would be even more unhappy than she is at present, her husband, in her interest and in that of her daughter, will never give his consent.   LIGNE.

" The Princess's diamonds and the rest of her property will be immediately returned to her, and she must send to Pradel the drawings belonging to her husband she still has in her possession."

Prince Charles wished to send back at once all the diamonds, furniture, and effects left by Hélène at Bel Œil and at Brussels, and he wrote to his mother urging her to forward them at once to their destination. It will be remembered that Hélène had left Brussels hurriedly at the time of the insurrec-

tion, and therefore had not had time to discharge a few personal debts contracted at her
own expense. The Princesse de Ligne wrote
to her daughter-in-law the following letter :—

BRUSSELS, 24*th February* 1791.

"As your husband had written to me,
Madame, that he consented to the return
of everything belonging to you, with the
exception of the books, most of which already
formed a part of the library at Bel Œil, the
rest having been purchased on condition of
their being placed in it, I was about to
order the packing of your effects when your
creditors, hearing of this, came to oppose
the proceedings, alleging that they never
received any answer to the letters they sent
you. They will not allow the removal of the
effects, which are their guarantee ; it is only
out of consideration for me, and on my
promising to write to you myself, that they
have consented to wait long enough for you
to receive this letter and send a reply.

" I therefore beg you, Madame, if you do not wish to run the risk of having your things publicly sold, to send me a bill of exchange or an order on some bank, so that by the end of April I may be able to meet their claims.

" The bills I have been able to collect, added to those I already know of, amount to about five thousand florins in our coin. As I do not intend to be in Brussels after the 15th of May, I warn you that unless I receive the money by the first of the month, I shall hand over your possessions to a public auctioneer, who will estimate their value and settle with the creditors, and I shall have nothing more to do with it. You will certainly not profit by this arrangement ; for I should have been more economical and have taken more interest in your affairs than he will.

" Sidonie is in excellent health; she is a dear little thing, and although you hardly notice her, she often speaks of you, and never forgets to mention her mother in her little prayers. Impatiently awaiting your reply, for, with the precautions I have taken, I am certain this letter will reach you, I remain, Madame, yours, etc.

"LA PRINCESSE DE LIGNE."

During these negotiations Hélène was living at Kowalowska in complete retirement. Her mother-in-law's letter arrived at a moment when it was impossible for her to send any money to Brussels. This woman of the world, accustomed to the most refined luxury, was almost in actual want, and with very natural pride would accept nothing from the Count but the hospitality he had offered her. She wrote to him as follows :—

"Your letter has made me very sad. There is no more question of your return than if you were never coming back. MM. de Ligne will listen to nothing; what can I do? What line of action can I take? What do they want of me? What is their object? They apparently hope that want will make me submit to their will, and imagine they are granting me a favour by shutting me up in a Convent with a pension.[1]   But even should they be willing to receive me back into their family, I would never return to them ; all is at an end between them and me, and I should even prefer the Convent to the trial of living with people whom I do not love, and who would despise me ; the word alone makes me shudder.

"As to the money question, it would be most painful to me to be a burden to anybody in the world ; I would sooner live by manual work, and would not hesitate to begin by discarding all my household, and keeping only one servant.

"The few effects I possess, such as books, music, and some pieces of furniture, I no longer consider as my own ; you will be good enough to take them into account in the sum

---

[1] This phrase shows that the Count had not sent Hélène the Prince's letter, in which he offered her one of his residences as a retreat.

I owe you for table expenses, washing, etc. ;
for, as regards money, I can give you none.
I have made a purchase this month, which I
should have avoided had I known my affairs
were in such a bad state.   I spent forty
ducats in buying linen to make chemises, for
I required some, and it was difficult for me to
do without them.   I was shown some fine
linen, and as it is often difficult to procure,
I bought it.   If I become a prey to absolute
misery, I shall yet have the necessary courage
to bear it.   You will care as much for me in
sackcloth as in silk, and I shall be quite happy.
I do not wish even to return into society.   I
became acquainted early in life with its most
brilliant attractions, and soon wearied of them;
I shall never get weary of a quiet life, even
attended with poverty, if you love me."

The Princesse Charles was a prey to all
kinds of anxiety ; her imagination was constantly inventing dangers : " I am far from
being reassured," she wrote to the Count ;
" on the contrary, it seems to me that each

moment increases my anxiety and worry.
I was told that on his return from Vienna the
Krajczy had gone to Dubus. If you meet
him I fear that he will encourage you to
separate from me ; he will certainly have
known MM. de Ligne at Vienna ; their
cause will have interested him, and he will
try to oblige them by urging you to abandon
me.   This idea tortures me.   Answer me
directly on this subject.   Since Thursday I
have been abandoned to the melancholy
tenure of my thoughts, and that without any
hope of consolation ; I am in great dread
lest your absence should be taken advantage
of to get you to give up all idea of our
union ; do not ever expect my consent to this.
Should it be necessary for your happiness, I
am ready to release you from your vows, but
nothing will induce me to break those by which
I have bound myself to love you always."

The Princess had received a very short
answer to the letter she had sent to the
Prince-Bishop.   He had not written himself,

but had replied through his steward that he would reflect on the subject, and that he refused for the time being to treat with his niece's delegate.   Hélène wrote to the Count, and added :—

" If my uncle will not abide by the settlement, he has only to cancel it, and give me back my lands.   But to take possession of my estates, and give me nothing in return, is really too unjust, and I cannot believe my uncle will let me die of hunger.   It would be infamous if, with the immense fortune I possess, I were reduced to poverty by so cruel an injustice, notwithstanding every law to the contrary.   God grant that I may escape the clutches of Silvestrowicz[1] with a sufficient income to be a burden to no one!   But where is my uncle?   Can I despatch any one to him, to explain my position and the ill-will of Silvestrowicz?   I shall find myself without a *sol*,[2] and then what shall I do? tell me.   But

---

[1] The Bishop of Wilna's steward.
[2] A halfpenny.

how could it be possible for my uncle to rob me so completely, without my obtaining any redress?   It is only in this country that such a thing could take place.   I am indeed very unhappy, but I am so affected by your absence that it prevents my dwelling upon my other griefs, which, at this moment, are but a minor part of my sorrows.   Good-bye, Vincent; love me, for your love is all I have left."

The Count had just arrived in Poland, but seemed in no hurry to return to Ukrania.

He wrote to Hélène that his own business kept him away from her, but that she had nothing to fear from the influences she had mentioned in a former letter.   " I am greatly relieved," she answers, "to hear at last that you are in Poland, and to know that I have nothing to fear from the *Krajczy;* his wife, his daughter, and his sons are all intimate friends of MM. de Ligne, and I dreaded lest he might meddle with our affairs.   As for myself, I consider the engagement which bound us to have been a fatal error, seeing we

were so young, and that our only fitness consisted in a mere similarity of birth and fortune.
To you alone I have given my pledge, my
real love, the most chaste and sacred of all
ties."

A short time after Hélène had fresh
cause for anxiety. " Fancy," she writes to the
Count, " I have read in the *Gazette de Ham-
bourg* that Prince Charles is about to return
to the Russian army by Léopol; he must
therefore pass by Niemirow, or at least quite
near it. I assure you that your Cossacks are
barely a sufficient protection to reassure a
coward like myself." [1]   But the Prince passed
through without troubling himself about her.

At last the Count announced his arrival.

---

[1] The Cossacks inhabited the plains of Ukrania, and the borders
of the Borysthenes (Dniester). These savage hordes, who lived by
plunder and pillage, were sometimes called Zaporogues (inhabitants
of the cataracts). Most of the Polish noblemen in this part of the
country had in their pay some hundreds of these brigands, who
caused the greatest terror. They belonged to those who paid them
best, and the cruelties committed by the Cossacks in Catherine's
pay during the massacres in Ukrania exceeded the greatest horrors
that can be imagined. (See, for more ample details, Comte de la
Garde's *Voyage in Ukrania.*)

"How my heart beats," writes Hélène, "when I think that the moment is drawing near which will bring you back to me. I am so taken up by your return that whether you have successfully or unsuccessfully settled my business is a question which does not interest me as it would at any other time. I count the minutes, and can only speculate on the hour at which you started, and the hour at which you may arrive, and it seems to me as though I had centuries to wait.

"I hope you will receive this letter on your way. I have just received one from my uncle; it appears that he *is not angry with me, and, with the exception of helping me by his influence or his money, is entirely devoted to me.* What irony! But what can I do? If my family is indifferent to me, I am quite the same towards them; provided that you always love me, I shall have no wish left in the world; I have neither vanity nor ambition, I have only love."

The Count arrived at Niemirow very much

dissatisfied with his journey, and anxious about the future. He had thought, from what Hélène had said, that he would meet with no opposition to a divorce on the part of the Lignes, and instead of the consent he expected, he had only received a very decided refusal, accompanied by a severe criticism of his own conduct, and of the interested motives which, rightly or wrongly, were attributed to him.

He had also fancied he would easily obtain his wife's consent by leaving her his two sons ; instead of this, his schemes were baffled on all sides by very serious difficulties.

On the other hand, the position of the Princess, who was living an isolated life, almost hidden, it may be said, in one of the Count's residences, in the neighbourhood of Niemirow, could no longer be endured without serious inconvenience. The Comtesse Anna was very much beloved in the country, her two children inhabited Niemirow, and everybody was beginning to wonder at her

prolonged absence; how much more extraordinary would it appear when her husband
should return! All these reflections threw
the Count into a gloomy state of mind;
he made a short stay at Kowalowska, but
Hélène was pained by the coldness of his
manner, and the embarrassment he showed
during their first interview; he briefly
narrated the unsatisfactory results of his
journey, intimating that he could not remain
at Niemirow, and advising her to go to her
uncle's and wait there for a solution which
was probably very remote.

Although the Count made these announce-
ments with a certain precaution, they pro-
duced a terrible impression on the Princess.
She had behaved with the utmost good faith,
persuaded that, to obtain a divorce and marry
directly after, was the easiest thing in the
world. Her marriage would cover the imprudence of her flight, and make every one
forget the conclusions they had drawn from
it. Suddenly she saw her dearest hopes

vanish, her honour compromised, and the
man for whom she had sacrificed everything
calmly suggest that she should leave him,
perhaps for ever. The strain on her over-
wrought mind was too great, and she fainted.
When she came to herself her women only
were around her bed, for the Count had
returned to Niemirow. She wrote to him at
once : " When you left me I was in the
greatest despair, yet you never showed the
slightest feeling of pity. I can only say that
I shall find my life odious if you persist in
your intention of abandoning me. I appeal
to you for an account of my destiny thus
committed to your charge. Is it possible you
could dispose of it with so little reflection ?"

Hélène in vain waited all day for a reply ;
the Count did not answer. The next day
she received a few lines, saying that he
was ill. The Princess was not in the habit
of leaving Kowalowska, and had never
entered the residence where the children of
the Countess Anna were living. But in her

anxiety she forgot all prudence, and wrote as follows : " I am in despair at hearing you are ill ; if you had sent me word sooner I should have perhaps found means of coming to see you. If you are unable to assist me otherwise, send me the key of the small garden gate ; Saint Charles will follow me, and I will come, for it is impossible for me to let to-day pass without seeing you ; I am in agony, and besides I have letters I must show you."

The Count's illness was only too genuine. The worry he had gone through during his journey, the awkwardness of his position, added to bodily fatigue, were probably its cause. At the end of three days a putrid fever of an alarming character declared itself, and for three months he was in danger of death.

The unhappy Hélène did not dare to take her place at his bedside ; she only went secretly to his room in order to be certain that every care was bestowed on him. The Bishop of Wilna, on hearing what was taking place, decided at last to write to his niece. He urged her to come and settle near him at Werky, and promised to forget her *past imprudences* if she would renounce her *mad infatuation for the Count.*

The Princess answered :—

" MY DEAR UNCLE—You must certainly have heard of the Lord Chamberlain's illness ; but what no one can tell you, and what I myself can hardly express, is the fearful state of despair I was in on seeing the only happiness possible for me in this world on the very brink of destruction.

" Now at last, after all my anxiety, he is out of danger, and although he was on the point of losing his life, I can truly assure you that he does not recover from a worse state than I do myself.

" Your letter arrived at the very moment that we were beginning to take courage, and to fancy that our union was still a possibility ; you will imagine my despair on · seeing that you only speak of a separation.

"I know your kindness of heart, my dear uncle, and am persuaded that you have never formed a plan without intending it to bring about my happiness and tranquillity ; I therefore implore you, my dear uncle, not to consider any plan feasible that should remove me or oblige me to forsake the choice I have made. Whatever reproach may be cast at me, I am certain I do not deserve to be blamed for want of firmness or constancy. I am quite decided not to change anything in my way of acting, even should the present impediments last as long as my life. I therefore beg you, my dear uncle, to vouchsafe me a few words of comfort. Tell me that you wish to see us happy, but do not tell us that we must seek our happiness apart from each other.

"Good-bye, my dear uncle ; accept the tribute of my deepest respect, and the tender affection which I shall bear you through life.

"HÉLÈNE LIGNE."

After a convalescence which lasted as long as his illness, the Count started for Galicia. He had been touched by Hélène's despair, and by her devotion to him. On leaving her he promised that he would again make every effort to obtain the divorce so ardently desired, and he left her, if not easy in her mind, at least somewhat reassured.

XII

Return of the Princes to Mons—Emigration in Belgium—A representation of *Richard Cœur de Lion*—Prince Charles re-enters the Austrian service—He represents the Emperor on his inauguration as Count of Hainault—War with France— Dumouriez in Champagne—The fight at Croix-aux-Bois— Death of Prince Charles—Despair of the Prince de Ligne.

THE pacification of Flanders was an accomplished fact, and in 1791 the Prince de Ligne, accompanied by Prince Charles, officially entered Mons as Grand Bailiff of Hainault. A magnificent banquet, followed by a concert and a ball, was given in their honour by the States of Hainault, in the Town Hall.[1]

Several poems were presented to the Prince de Ligne by the students of the college of Houdain and others. It is unnecessary to say that the virtues of the

---

[1] The expenses of this banquet amounted to nine thousand eight hundred and ninety-five livres. (*Archives of Mons.*)

Prince and the glory of his son were the chosen theme.

However, in the midst of this concert of praise, one discordant note was heard.   A certain lawyer from Nivelle, called Masson, published a libel on the occasion.   " Amongst several other things I have forgotten," writes the Prince, " he said that at my entry as governor of Hainault I looked like an old Sultan, surrounded by women, to whom I devoted the whole of my attention, and that I had been stupid enough to accept in good faith acclamations of ' Long live the Patriot Prince.'   This last statement is true.   It was in a church, where I was either taking or administering the oath.   I accepted this cry with the rest, without suspecting that its utterer had any malicious intention.   As for the Sultan, he does me too much honour ; it is true that, during my tedious progress, some very pretty girls threw bouquets into my carriage, and the crowd obliging them to stop near the door, I thanked them very much,

and told them they were charming. The
only reproach which might be considered not
quite unfounded was that concerning my
entry. The war had just ended, as well as
the rebellion in the Netherlands, both of
which had cost me a great deal of money.
I might have made debts and covered my
followers with gold lace ; but I thought, on
the contrary, the people would be grateful to
me for not making too great a display. As
I had two Turks, four Hussars, several
bearded Russians, a Tartar with two dromedaries, and a Turkish band, he might very
well compare me to Tamerlane or the Emperor of China, though I do not remember
exactly which of the two I was supposed
to resemble."

The Princes were very heartily received
by the inhabitants of the good town of Mons,
where they were much beloved ; on the following day they started with their family for Bel
Œil.

As soon as he was settled the first thing

the Prince did was to erect a monument in honour of his beloved son Charles, to perpetuate
the memory of his brilliant conduct at Sabacz
and at Ismaïl.   He designed it himself, chose
the site, and laid it out so as to imitate a spot
in the Empress's gardens at Czarskoë-Celo.
" By following the left bank of the river," he
says, "you come upon an obelisk dedicated by
Friendship to Valour.   It is not my fault if
Charles is the hero of it; it is not my fault if
Charles distinguished himself in the war ; it
is not my fault if I am the father of such a
perfect being.   The father disappears, the
man remains, and the hero is celebrated ; I
must not be accused of partiality, but I may
be accused of pride."

This obelisk, in marble, is forty-five feet
high.   On one side is inscribed, in gold
letters, the following : " To my dear Charles,
for Sabacz and Ismaïl ; " on the second,
" *Nec te juvenis memorande silebo ;* " and on
the third, " His glory is my pride, his friendship my happiness."

The de Lignes spent the summer at Bel
Œil, happy to be quiet and united once more
in the country they loved so well ; but to an
attentive observer the tranquillity which
reigned in Flanders was not to be of long
duration ; threatening symptoms might be
discerned on every side. The frightful progress of the French revolution, and the
presence of the *émigrés* in the Netherlands,
caused anxiety in many minds.

Savoy, Switzerland, the Black Forest,
Liege, Treves, Luxemburg, and the Netherlands were the first asylums of the persecuted ;
it was only later on, when they had lost all
hope of a speedy return, that they went to
Vienna, London, Poland, and Russia. The
Archduchess Marie Christine, regent in the
Netherlands, was the sister of the Queen of
France ; it was natural she should protect the
émigrés ; but Leopold was not favourably
disposed towards them, and in the very beginning of his reign he requested the Archduchess Christine and the Electors of

Mayence, Cologne, and Treves to do all in
their power to prevent the refugees and the
Princes from doing anything rash.   " Do not
allow yourselves to be led into anything,"
he wrote ; "do nothing the French or the
Princes ask you to do ; meet them with
civilities and dinners, but give them neither
troops, money, nor help of any sort."   He
entirely separated the cause of the King
from that of the *émigrés*.

The Prince de Ligne was extremely ill-
disposed towards the Emperor Leopold ; he
reproached him with having sucked the milk
of Italian dissimulation, and he would not
have anything to do with his pretended
political calculations.   He adored the Queen,
and his heart leaped with indignation at the
thought of the dangers which daily threatened her more and more.

He had vainly solicited a command in
the Austrian army.   Leopold had carefully
avoided granting his request, for he feared
the imprudences his vivacity, his opinions,

and his chivalrous devotion might lead him to commit.

We must admit that the Prince de Ligne was no passionate admirer of liberty ; he very soon foresaw the tendencies of the revolution, and in 1790 wrote to the Comte de Ségur concerning the National Assembly : " Greece had her philosophers, but they were only seven ; you have twelve hundred of them at eighteen francs a day, having no mission but what they arrogate to themselves, no knowledge of foreign countries, no general plan of operations, and not even the sea, which is a sort of protection to the makers of empty phrases, and to the laws of the country it surrounds."

The Prince never missed an opportunity of showing his sympathy for the royal family. One day he was present at a representation of *Richard Cœur de Lion* at the small theatre at Tournai. The public was chiefly composed of French *émigrés*, who were full of hope and illusion, impatiently awaiting the time when they should return to their country.   The Prince could not hear without emotion the air of: *O Richard! Ô mon roi! l'univers t'abandonne.*[1] Tears came into his eyes, and the audience, perceiving his emotion, frantically applauded. "At that part," says the Prince, "where the promise is made to avenge the poor captive king, I advanced, applauding as though I too wished to contribute my efforts.   I was in earnest at the time, and it seemed likely that my services would be accepted.   Suddenly the French ladies, both young and old, in the excitement rushed out of their boxes, and the whole of the pit, mostly consisting of young French officers, jumped on the stage, crying out: 'Long live the King!   Long live the Prince de Ligne;' and they only stopped clapping their hands to wipe their eyes overflowing with tears."

Among the young refugee officers who

---

[1] Oh Richard ! oh my King ! the whole world forsakes thee.

were the most cordially received at Bel Œil
was M. de Villeneuve Laroche.   He writes
in his Memoirs :[1]   " The Prince de Ligne at
this time was residing with all his family at
Bel Œil, a fine estate distant one league from
the town of Ath ; he took pleasure in con-
versing with us about the principles of honour
that were the basis of our conduct, and he
commended us with enthusiasm.

   " He was good enough to invite me several
times to dine at his magnificent residence ; I
may even go so far as to say that I formed
quite an intimacy with his eldest son, Prince
Charles, an officer of the very greatest
promise ; he was a *colonel major* in the
artillery, and had lately distinguished himself
in the war against the Turks. . . .

   " The son sympathised with our feelings as
much as his father.   He told me one day
that he had just written to the Emperor
asking to be employed in the coalition war,

---

[1] Villeneuve Laroche, *Memoirs on Quiberon.*

and added that if his request was rejected he would serve as a mere volunteer with the French nobility."

Prince Charles had in fact urgently requested to be allowed to return to the Austrian army, with the rank of colonel in the engineers. After the death of the Emperor Leopold, which took place on the 27th of February 1792, the Prince was given an appointment in General Clairfayt's army corps. The Austrian general-in-chief was the Duke Albert of Saxe-Teschen, husband of the Archduchess Christine.

The campaign was opened against the armies of the French republic; and already, on the 27th of May, Prince Charles had distinguished himself by his daring valour in a fight that took place near Condé; but no great battle was yet imminent. The enemy confined himself to skirmishes; the Duke Albert's headquarters were at Mons, and the inauguration of the new Emperor, François II., as Count of Hainault, was to take place in that town. Prince Charles de Ligne was chosen to represent the sovereign on this occasion.[1]

We read in the *Journal du Palais et historique* of the councillor Paridaens the following paragraph :—

7*th June* 1792.

"This day being a feast of the Holy Sacrament, his Royal Highness the Duke Albert of Saxe-Teschen, who is Governor-General of the Netherlands, followed in the procession. Several generals accompanied him—among others, the Prince de Lambesc, of the House of Lorraine, who had been transferred from the French to the Austrian service, and also the son of the Prince de Ligne."

---

[1] On the 11th June 1792 the inauguration of the Emperor François II. took place at Mons. By letters patent granted at Vienna on the 19th March, the new Emperor had authorised the Duc Albert de Saxe-Teschen to represent him in this ceremony, and to take the customary oaths in his name. The Duke Albert having in his turn appointed the Prince de Ligne, Grand Bailiff of Hainault, to perform these duties, the latter conferred the honour on Prince Charles, his eldest son. (Note communicated by M. Deviller, keeper of the records at Mons.)

9th June.

"On this day, Saturday, the Prince de Ligne's son, although quartered for some time at Mons, made his official entry into the town as Commissary to his Majesty at the ceremony of Inauguration which is to take place on the day after to-morrow. Guns were fired, although we are at the very seat of war. He entered on horseback by the Havré gate, crossed the square, and went up the Rue Neuve to the hôtel de Ligne,[1] while the bells were ringing. He was followed by the dragoon officers of the Coburg regiment, and by his liveried retainers.

"However, as the French, who were camped at Maubeuge, showed a disposition to interfere in the ceremony of Inauguration, and had in the last few days drawn nearer towards Petit, Quévy, and even Bougnies, on the evening of the 10th of June an attack was pre-

---

[1] The hôtel de Ligne was on the Rue de la Grosse Pomme, it is now a hospital for incurables.

pared and carried out at two o'clock in the morning. There was a violent onset and sharp cannonading, which lasted till five."

Prince Charles, who would not have missed this fight for anything in the world, started off in the middle of the night at the head of his regiment, despite the Archduke Albert's opposition. He fought with his usual bravery, was very nearly taken prisoner, having imprudently ventured too far amidst the enemy; and at seven in the morning, black with powder and heated with the fight, he arrived on horseback, post haste, barely in time to put on his full dress uniform and get into his coach.

The ceremony of the Emperor's Inauguration as Count of Hainault is as old as the days of Charlemagne, but this was the last time that the traditional custom was to be celebrated. We have seen the importance attached to it by the States of Hainault at the time of the Flemish insurrection.

At half-past eight all the clergy of Mons, the ladies of the Chapter of Sainte Waudru, following the shrine of the saint, who was the patroness of Mons, all the magistrates, the deputies of the town council, the chief councillor of the Provinces in his State robes, and the twenty-six deputies of the chief towns in Hainault, preceded by magnificent banners from all the parishes, embroidered in gold and silk, took their places in the theatre. At nine o'clock his Highness the Prince Charles de Ligne left his hotel in a coach drawn by six horses and preceded by a detachment of dragoons, by the members of the order of the nobility, each one in a coach drawn by two horses, and by a herald-at-arms on horseback, named O'Kelly, bearing his coat-of-arms, and the cap and wand of his office. The guards and officers of his house closed the procession. On reaching the theatre his Highness seated himself on an arm-chair under a canopy, above which was placed a portrait of his Majesty.

When all the different orders were placed and seated, the trumpets sounded, Murray's regiment fired a volley of musketry, the artillery on the ramparts answered by a salute, and the herald-at-arms, advancing to the front of the theatre, called *Silence* three times. Then the Prince rose, and, laying his hand on the Gospels, first took the oath to the Chapter of Sainte Waudru, of which he was named Abbot. The Princesse de Croy, first lady of the Chapter, presented to him the crozier, and a salute of artillery and music and trumpets, etc., announced to the people that the first act of the ceremony had taken place. The Prince afterwards took the oath to the States, in the same manner; and finally, a third time to the town of Mons, after which he solemnly received the oaths of allegiance from the said Chapter, States, and Town.

"During the ceremony," says the councillor Paridaens, "some national guards, taken prisoners in that night's encounter, had been brought to the square, and just as the procession was threading its way to Sainte Waudru, at the entrance of the road, it was met by the generals who were returning from fighting the French. At the head of these generals was the Duc Albert de Saxe, with his nephew the Archduke Charles,[1] who had been under fire for the first time in his life. At that very moment the news arrived that M. de Gouvion, Commander-in-Chief of the French army, had been killed. It was vaguely known that the French had been repulsed, after having made, however, a good stand for the first time. Indeed the cannon had been heard without interruption from two o'clock till six in the morning. On the 12th of June H.R.H. Madame arrived about ten o'clock in the morning. "On entering the rooms of the Government House she heartily and re-

---

[1] The Archduke Charles-Louis, born in 1771, and youngest brother of the Emperor François, was one of the best Austrian generals during Napoleon's wars; it is rather curious to study the outset of his military career.

peatedly embraced her nephew, the Archduke
Charles, as one might a friend whom one
sees for the first time after he has encount-
ered a great danger.   I saw this from my
dining-room windows."

The Prince gave a banquet that evening to
the principal town authorities; the Archdukes,
the Prince de Lambesc, and other generals
were present.   On the following day he returned to the camp, only too glad to have
done with a part so little in keeping with his
natural modesty.   Two months went by,
events were succeeding each other in France
with the most startling rapidity, the position
of the royal family was becoming daily more
critical, till the terrible 10th of August induced
the Duke of Brunswick, commander-in-chief
of the allied forces, to alter his plan of campaign.   He decided to move on the army in
the direction of the gorge of Argonne, so as
to enter Champagne by Sainte Menehould,
and march on Paris by Châlons.   He gave
orders to General Clairfayt to join him with

twenty-five thousand men, who were to form the right wing of his army. This change of position on the part of Count Clairfayt decided Dumouriez, then at the camp of Maulde, to proceed to the plains of Champagne with the greater part of his army.

During the three months that had elapsed since the inauguration at Mons no important battle had afforded Prince Charles an opportunity of distinguishing himself; but, gifted with a sound judgment and an observant mind, he had employed the interval in forming a just estimate of the illusions entertained by the *émigrés*, and of the very imperfect description they had given of the state of France. He wrote from the camp at Boux a letter, which fell into the hands of the republicans, and was read at a public sitting of the Convention.[1]

"We are beginning to get tired of

---

[1] *Moniteur*, "Sitting of the Convention," Thursday evening, 27th September 1792.

this war, in respect of which MM. *les émigrés* had promised us more butter than bread. We have to fight against troops of the line who never desert, and national troops who remain at their posts. The peasants, who are armed, fire on our men, and if one of them is found alone or asleep in a house he is murdered. The weather, since our entry into France, has been horrible; it rains in torrents every day, and the roads are so bad that at the present moment we cannot move our cannon; moreover, we are almost in a state of famine. We have the greatest difficulty in obtaining bread for the soldiers, and meat is often wanting; many of the officers remain for five or six days without warm food. Our shoes and cloaks are rotten, and our men are beginning to fall ill; the villages are deserted, and provide neither vegetables, nor brandy, nor flour; I do not know what we shall do, nor what will become of us."

This letter expresses a discouragement

that must have been general, and circumstances were favourable to Dumouriez in
preparing for the attack ; but it was indispen-
sable that he should at any cost prevent the
allied army from occupying the Argonne pass.
The forest was impenetrable except by five
passages, which it was necessary to guard
and hold against the enemy.   These passes
were the Chêne-Populeux, the Croix-au-Bois,
the Grand-Pré, the Chalade and the Islettes.
A camp placed at the Islettes and a position
taken up at the Chalade would close the two
principal roads to Clermont and to Var-
ennes, and General Dillon was despatched
for the purpose.   Dumouriez established himself at Grand-Pré, to close the roads to
Rheims and to the Croix-au-Bois.   He sent
orders to General Duval, then at Pont-sur-
Sambre, to break up his camp at once and
advance by forced marches to the pass of the
Chêne-Populeux.

Dumouriez felt certain of success, but an
act of imprudence frustrated his hopes.

The pass of the Croix-au-Bois had been considered less important than the others, and was only defended by a couple of battalions of infantry and two squadrons of cavalry. Dumouriez, in the stress of the moment, had not had the time to see and judge personally of the importance of this pass, but the German spies, employed to inspect the different French posts, informed the Duke of Brunswick of the advantages of this badly-guarded pass. Clairfayt confided the attack to Prince Charles de Ligne, who started on the 13th of September at early dawn to seize it. The abatis intended to bar the road had been carelessly made, the half-buried branches not offering any resistance to the enemy; the imperialists easily forced a passage, and the roads had been so slightly damaged that they made their way at once. They met with hardly any resistance, and easily carried the position. The men who held it hastily fell back on Dumouriez's camp; the latter, anxious at the

turn things were taking, immediately despatched two brigades of infantry, and six
squadrons of cavalry, to General Chazot, with
orders to recapture the pass at any cost.
Chazot spent the day without attacking, but,
on receiving fresh and urgent orders to risk
an attack, he opened fire on the morning of
the 14th.

The attack and the defence were vigorous ;
six times the post was carried by the
French, and as often recaptured by the
Austrians.   Prince Charles sees that in order
to keep the position it is necessary to capture
a French battery, which, cleverly placed, is
inflicting heavy losses on the Austrians.   A
vigorous charge is necessary ; the Prince
in person leads the attack on the battery ;
eight men in the front rank are shot dead.
He dashes forward himself, the ninth,
but, shot through the head by a bullet, he
reels for a moment in the saddle, and falls
back dead.

The French regained possession of the

pass, and raised the body of the unfortunate Prince. They found two gold chains with a locket round his neck, and in his pocket an unfinished letter.

Clairfayt, in despair at the cruel loss the army had sustained, hastened to avenge it, and took possession of the Croix-au-Bois.

He immediately claimed the body of the Prince, and it was at once given up. Mass was celebrated in the camp the following morning, and the coffin started for Mons. At that moment M. de Villeneuve Laroche, a guest at Bel Œil, and a friend of Prince Charles, arrived on the scene.

"On the battlefield," he says, "where yesterday the republicans were defeated, I met a funeral procession, escorted by a few foreign troops, going in the direction of Hainault. It was that of the young Prince de Ligne, who was killed in the fight, and the body was being taken to his unhappy father at Bel Œil."

Prince Charles's death was universally deplored ; his brilliant military qualities caused him to be regretted by the whole army ; the Baron de Breteuil wrote from Verdun to the Comte de Fersen : " Yesterday Clairfayt's army came in for a sharp fight at the outposts, in which, however, it was victorious. Clairfayt's army lost in the attack five or six hundred men, but what deeply affects me is that Prince Charles de Ligne was killed. I loved him from a child ; he was the most distinguished amongst the Austrians of the same age. His father will feel the loss terribly."

Prince Charles's body was conveyed to Bel Œil, after passing through Mons[1] at night, but his father was no longer there ; he had been recalled, with Marshal de Lascy, to Vienna.

When the terrible news arrived no one dared to tell him of it, and the Marshal alone had the courage to undertake the delicate mission. He sent the Prince word that he had received

---

[1] Forty years ago, at Mons, there were old men who remembered Prince Charles's death as an event which afflicted the whole city.

bad news from Clairfayt's army, adding that
he would himself come and inform him of it.
"My son is wounded!" said the Prince as
the Marshal entered. The latter remained
silent. "But speak, good God! . . ."—
"Alas! I would not, or I could not, understand," he writes, "when he said that dreadful word : *Dead !* . . . I feel crushed by the
news, and he had almost to carry me away
in his arms. I see it still, the spot where I
was when the Marshal told me that my poor
Charles was killed ; I see my poor Charles
himself, as he welcomed me every day with
the sunshine of his happy and good face. I
had dreamt a few days before that he had
received a mortal wound in the head, and had
fallen dead from his horse. For five or six
days I was anxious, but as one always treats
as a weakness that which is often a warning,
or perhaps a feeling of nature when there are
ties of blood, I cast from my thoughts the
fatal foreboding which was only too soon to
be realised!"

The Prince never got over his son's
death, and he entirely lost all enjoyment in
life.   This sad recollection had made in his
heart a deep and incurable wound.   " That
so light-hearted a man," says Count Ouvaroff,
" who had lived through so much and was so
careless of misfortune, should ten years after
this calamity break down at the bare mention
of the beloved name!   No one dared utter
it in his presence ; if he happened to speak
of his son his voice would betray the
intensity of his grief, and his eyes fill
with tears."   There is something strangely
touching in this picture of the old man,
formerly so worldly and sceptical, as we
should say nowadays, who *would not be
comforted* because he still thought of the
child of his heart who was no longer.
" There is," said the Prince with admirable
philosophy, when shortly after he lost all
his fortune, "there is a terrible method of
rising above circumstances.   It is bought
at the cost of a great grief.   If the soul

has been wounded by the loss of all that
is dearest, I defy minor misfortunes to
touch it; loss of wealth, total ruin, per-
secutions, injustice, everything sinks into
insignificance."

XIII

Prince Charles's will—Hélène receives the news of her husband's death—Departure for Werky—Hélène marries Count Potocki.

THE unhappy Prince de Ligne had immediately sent to Bel Œil the necessary instructions for his son's last wishes to be fulfilled, but the victory of Jemappes, which ceded the whole of Belgium to the French, prevented the de Ligne family from returning to Bel Œil, now in the hands of the enemy. Prince Charles's wishes were contained in a will written shortly before his death. We shall see that he instinctively felt he would fall a victim in the course of this war. Perhaps, indeed, weary of life, he sought death, for he seemed to brave it; at all events the deepest melancholy overshadows the following pages :—

Prince Charles de Ligne's Will.

"As I shall most probably be killed, if not in this war at least in some other, I wish my body to be recovered and my funeral to be conducted with all the honours of war, and with the greatest pomp—military, of course.

"I wish my body to be carried to Bel Œil, after having been embalmed, so as not to incommode any one, for I desire to be laid with my good ancestors, who from father to son have all been honest men.

"I desire that my heart be wrapped up separately in a handkerchief which shall have belonged to her I love, and which I beg her to give for that purpose. As she has always possessed my heart during my lifetime, I wish it, after my death, to be as happy as a heart can be in the absence of the beloved one, that is to say, in company with something that has been her's. I beg her to embroider on the first corner of the handkerchief *Alona ;*

on the second *Tendresse delicieuse;* on the third *Indissoluble;* and on the fourth the 21st September 1787, and the date of my death.

"I.—The whole of my collection of engravings, my collection of original drawings, and in general all the contents of my portfolios, are to be sold to the best purchaser. One will have to see in what country the sale will be most advantageous, whether in Paris, Vienna, London, or Amsterdam.

"*Nota bene.*—Should any of my family wish to have these, he can take them at the estimated value, which, however, cannot be less than a hundred thousand German florins; for the drawings are really priceless, as I have none of inferior value, and all are recognised originals. This will, therefore, bring in a clear sum of a hundred thousand florins, which will be completely my own, and quite independent of the succession due to my natural heirs, which I leave to them according to law. This sum of a hundred thousand florins is to be divided into two parts : eighty thousand are to be sunk in an annuity for the benefit of my natural daughter Christine, so that there will be eight thousand florins a year for her keep and education, which, up to the age of fifteen, may be five hundred florins, and a thousand florins up to the age of twenty, at which time she will probably be married, and can then spend her money as she chooses : In such a manner, however, that she shall not spend more than eight thousand florins ; and that all the money saved on this sum, up to the age of twenty or five-and-twenty, if she does not marry before, shall be placed out at four or five per cent interest; this will become her children's property, care being taken always to add the interest to the capital.

"II.—Should she die without children, Norokos is to be her heir. As I am the adopted father of Norokos, the Turkish child I found abandoned during the war, the remaining sum of twenty thousand florins out of the hundred thousand realised by the sale shall be sunk in the same way on his account. The directions as to its use are the same as for little Christine. Should he die without children, Christine is to be his heir. I recommend their marrying, if they have any inclination one for the other; it is my greatest wish, and I beg my sister Christine to encourage this. I appoint her their guardian, and in default of my sister Christine, I appoint Madame la Comtesse Thérèse Dietrichstein, formerly married to Comte de Kinsky. I bequeath also to little Christine the portrait of her mother, painted by Le Clerc, and the chain I wear round my neck, with the following words on the clasps: 'Ces liens me sont chers' (these ties are precious to me). I beg her never to part with it, but always to wear it as a remembrance of myself and of the person who gave it to me.

" III.—My dispositions for the servants.

" I bequeath to Norokos my damaskeened

Turkish gun with gold mountings, and my sabre with the steel guard—the one I carried during this war, in order that he may remember that it is to war he owes his condition; that he must look upon a military career as his fortune, his element; and upon the army as his country.

"IV.—I bequeath to my father the small painting by Le Clerc and M. Duvivier's drawing, both representing the fight at Pösig, and I beg that my crosses of the orders of Merit and that of Saint George be suspended from them, since I won them by my father's example; and as also I owe the happiness of having acquired some friends in the army through listening to all Lieutenant Wolff said to my father when dying, and remembering it all my life.

"V.—I bequeath to my sister Christine all my framed drawings, with the miniatures, cameos, and small frames.

"VI.—I bequeath to my daughter Sidonie her mother's portrait, so that she may re-

member not to follow her example, and the
Turkish sabre given me by Prince Potemkin,
which she is always to keep in her room,
so that her children may understand that I
intend them to become soldiers ; when her
son fights his first battle, in which, I trust,
he will distinguish himself, she will give him
this sabre from me.

" VII.—I bequeath to Madame de Kinsky,
who was Countess Dietrichstein by birth, all
the framed engravings I have in my apartment at Bel Œil, and also the chain I wear
round my neck which was given me by her
dearest friend ; I venture, on this account, to
beg that she will wear it all her life, in
remembrance of one whose happiness was
bound up with that of Madame de Kinsky ;
this I positively affirm.

" VIII. — I bequeath to Madame la
Princesse de Lichtenstein, a Mandesch by
birth, several things I have at Brussels,
which will be described later on, and besides
these my watch, as a token that the happiest

hours it has told are those I spent with her,
and that to the very last I thought of her as
a friend whose place in my heart was next to
the one I have always adored.

"IX.—I bequeath to the Princess Jablonowska, Countess Czaski by birth, several
things I have at Brussels, which will hereafter
be named, and also the ring I always wear
with the motto ' Indissoluble,' the small port-
folio with the chain, and the other portfolios
or caskets containing letters and manuscripts
written by myself. I give this last proof
of my confidence to her who has most
claims on my gratitude for past kindness,
who has best understood the nature of my
thoughts, of my troubles,—in short, to a true
friend, whom I am sure not to forget even in
the other world.

"X.—I bequeath to the Princess Linowska,
Thun by birth, my fine edition of Shake-
speare's works, and the best English horse in
my stable, on condition that it will be kept
exclusively for her use.

"XI.—I bequeath to Mademoiselle Caroline de Thun my eight handsome silver candlesticks, and my handsome coffee-pot, and besides this an annuity of twenty ducats, in order that she may procure for herself wherever she goes, and even in the house which she most frequents, the best arm-chair or couch that can possibly be made.

"XII.—I bequeath to Madame de Woina[1] a table and a tea-service, in order that she may remember the pleasure I had in going to take tea with her; also two Turkish sabres for her children, Maurice and Felix.

"XIII.—I bequeath to my good friend Poniatowski, my sabre set with Marshal Laudon's stone, and also the shoulder belt, requesting him to wear it should he meet the enemy, in honour of one who to save his life would willingly have sacrificed his own. Also my fine horse Winer, so that he may be cared for all his life.

---

[1] These three ladies were sisters.

"XIV.—I bequeath to my brother Louis the King of Poland's sabre and Marlborough's pistols.

"XV.—I bequeath to my friend François, Comte de Dietrichstein, the arms found with me if I am killed, or that belong to me should I die a natural death, excepting those disposed of by special legacies; I beg him to collect and distribute the above-named legacies, and I am certain that he will not leave my body to the enemy. Should, however, an accident intervene, such as his being wounded himself, he must neglect nothing in having it reclaimed, with the chains and other things I wear on my person.

"XVI.—The portraits of Mesdames de Kinsky, Lichtenstein, Jablonowska, Linowska, and Caroline, as well as Poniatowski's and that of Madame de Woina, which I request may be obtained, shall be placed in my apartment in the tower at Bel Œil, where I have already placed the coloured prints belonging to Madame de Kinsky. My wife's portrait is to be previously removed and placed in the lumber-room. This chamber is to become a Temple to Friendship, and over the door shall be inscribed the words : *Abode of the insepar-able.*

" I request that my bust shall be placed on a pedestal in the centre of the tower, and turned in the direction of Madame de Kinsky's portrait, and I beg my father to compose and have engraved on this pedestal some verses describing the happiness I have enjoyed in her society ; but they must not contain any praise of myself ; under each portrait he will write in verse a description of the person represented.

" XVII.—Arrangements for my household (not copied).

" XVIII.—I bequeath to Madame de Kinsky my good dog Tristan, that he may be taken good care of ; he has been treated by me as I was by her, like a good and ever-faithful dog."

Note added by the Countess Dietrichstein.— " The body was embalmed, and, considering the circumstances, sent to Bel Œil by mail coach. A Mass was said at the headquarters at Boux, in the presence of all the officers; and orders were given that the last honours should be rendered to his memory on the passage of the coffin through Mons, where he was well known and beloved.

" In order to carry out his wishes as much as possible, the handkerchief will be placed in his coffin; the date he asks for is unfortunately from the 21st of September 1787 to the 14th of September 1792."

Notwithstanding the mysterious reserve with which the Prince expresses himself, it is difficult not to believe that Madame de Kinsky was the secret object of his deep attachment. On reading his last wishes, so imbued with nobleness, tenderness, and generosity, we wonder how Hélène could have so misunderstood him, and obliged him as it were to transfer his affection to another. Perhaps she was not entirely responsible for their disunion; a mother or a friend like

Madame de Rochechouart might have guarded her at the outset from many an imprudent step. It was impossible to expect experience and wisdom in a child of fifteen. During the last two years she had begun to feel how dearly they are purchased.

All this time Hélène had remained alone at Kowalowska. Notwithstanding the imprudences her passion for the Count had led her to commit, she had never for one moment entertained any other idea than that of marriage, though she knew in what light her conduct was judged by the world.

Mortified and discouraged, Hélène was giving herself up to the gloomiest ideas, when she suddenly received the news of her husband's death. The sudden transition from despair to joy stunned her at first ; but soon only one feeling possessed her soul, that of her freedom, and she hurriedly wrote these few lines to the Count :—

"A cannon-ball has carried off Prince Charles. I am free ; it is God's will : *This cannon was loaded from all eternity!"*[1]   And absorbed in the selfishness of her passion, she did not for one instant regret the first companion of her life, or shed a tear for the father of her child.   His glorious and touching end did not inspire her with an atom of pity.

And then, as if, indeed, death had received from God the mission of removing all possible obstacles to Hélène's happiness, a few days later the second son of the Countess Anna died of a gangrenous sore throat, before his unhappy mother was able to reach him ; and that nothing might be wanting to complete the romance, the Princess heard almost at the same moment of the death of her brother Xavier, leaving her heiress to an income of six hundred thousand livres.[2]

The Count had reached Niemirow in time to see his son, of whom, it must be added, Hélène had taken the utmost care.   He wrote

---

[1] These were the words Madame de Sévigné used when writing to Bussy Rabutin on the death of Turenne.

[2] Twenty-four thousand pounds.

in all haste to the Countess Anna to tell her the fatal news, and then in another letter he announced to her Prince Charles's death, and offered to give her back at once her eldest son, François, in exchange for her consent to their divorce. The unfortunate woman resisted no longer, she only begged that the legal forms should be carefully observed in obtaining the consent of the Court of Rome, hoping that in the interval her husband might return to her before the last step was taken. Directly after his mother's answer the little Count François, accompanied by his governess and servants, started to meet her.

Without loss of time Hélène wrote to her uncle, whose character she well understood; she told him of her husband's death, and implored his aid for the settlement of her brother's affairs; she ended by asking him to see Count Vincent, who would be able to explain many important details difficult to negotiate in writing. She sent this letter to the Prince-Bishop by Major Hoffman, a

Polish gentleman attached to the service of the Lord Chamberlain.

The embassy was a complete success. The prelate, calculating that Count Vincent Potocki living would be infinitely more useful to him than the Prince de Ligne dead, wrote to the Count, and begged him to come and see him when he should next go to Warsaw, and in the meanwhile offered to receive his niece at Werky. Hélène sent the following reply :—

December 1792.

"MY VERY DEAR AND VERY HONOURED UNCLE—It is with the deepest gratitude that I received through Major Hoffman the assurance of your paternal disposition towards me. It has awakened in me the warmest and strongest feelings. Pray receive, my dear uncle, my compliments and my thanks. Many things at present prevent my going to see you as I should wish, but as soon as, by the grace of God, I am able to do so, I shall have the honour of presenting myself

XIII PRINCESSE DE LIGNE 273

in person, and reiterating to you the deep respect with which I have the honour to subscribe myself, my very dear and revered uncle, your very humble and obedient servant and niece,

" Hélène Massalska,

" Dowager-Princesse de Ligne."

Then she wrote to the Count Vincent : " I do not advise you to await the arrival of the Prince-Bishop before writing to him, for he is one of those persons who never know when they will start or when they will arrive. You could send a messenger to Werky, who would wait for an answer, which might per- haps hurry on matters ; but if the Prince- Bishop could see you, he would do every thing you wish, and we should be happy."

The Count did not make up his mind to go, and Hélène, fearing his capricious and irresolute character, went to Werky her- self. She entreated her uncle to apply to the Pope, so as to hasten the formalities necessary for the divorce, for she was in

daily fear that the project on which she had
set her heart should fall through.

Everything took place in accordance with
the Princess's wishes, and *three months* after
the death of Prince Charles de Ligne the
marriage of Hélène and Count Potocki was
celebrated at midnight in the Chapel of the
Convent of the Bernadines near Werky.
The apparent motive of this secrecy was the
Princess's mourning, as yet too recent to
allow of an official wedding ; but it must be
added that the permission for a divorce had
not yet arrived from Rome, and only came
three months later. It required all the influence of the Prince-Bishop to obtain a priest
that should celebrate the marriage under such
conditions.

On entering the Chapel, and at the moment
of realising the happiness she so ardently desired, Hélène experienced the deepest emotion, mingled with a vague sense of terror. She
knelt beside the Count, and remained motion-
less, her eyes fixed on the ground, and ab-

sorbed in her thoughts. When the Count gave her his hand to lead her to the altar she rose to her feet, but suddenly stopped short, with a fixed and terrified gaze, a prey to the most terrible hallucination. By the flickering light of the wax tapers she fancied she saw three coffins laid across her path, which she would have to step over on her way to the altar. The Count, appalled at Hélène's terrified look, inquired in a low voice the cause of her alarm; the sound of his voice recalled her to herself, and, chasing away the horrible vision by a strong effort of will, she resolutely ascended the three steps of black marble, which a moment before had presented such a sinister appearance. The bridal pair returned to Werky, and the terrible moment was soon forgotten.

After a prolonged stay in Lithuania, during which the Lord Chamberlain visited his wife's extensive domains, they both returned to Ukrania, and Hélène triumphantly entered the Count's abode, whither she had gone in

such fear and trembling at the time of his illness.   The past and all its sorrows were forgotten, and, radiant with happiness, she wrote
to her husband, who was absent for a few days :
" To-morrow I shall see you again, and see
you still the same, for I do not want you ever
to change in the smallest degree : virtues,
attractions, wit, faults, caprices, all are
precious to me ; if you were more perfect,
you would no longer be the Vincent for whose
sake I should have been guilty of the greatest
folly, if kind heaven had not permitted that
all should be for the best in the end."

THE END

Printed by R. & R. CLARK, *Edinburgh.*

S. & H.

www.ingramcontent.com/pod-product-compliance
Lightning Source LLC
Chambersburg PA
CBHW021049030726
47496CB00006B/1749